Entwined Publishing books by K.E. Turner

The Wolves of Langeias
Wolf's Keep
Wolf's Prize
Wolf's Redemption

The Descendants
The Wolf and His Witch

The Descendants

THE WOLF AND HIS WITCH

K.E. TURNER

ENTWINED PUBLISHING

The Wolf and His Witch
ISBN # 978-1-80250-251-0
©Copyright K.E. Turner 2025
Cover Art by Kelly Martin ©Copyright July 2025
Interior text design by Entwined Publishing
Published by Eternal, an Entwined Publishing imprint

Published in 2025 by Entwined Publishing, United Kingdom.

Entwined Publishing is a division of Totally Entwined Group Limited.

THE WOLF AND HIS WITCH

Dedication

To my brother, Mitch,
who loves it when his wife reads spicy romances.
You're welcome.

Author's Note

Dear Reader,

When I encounter foreign words I do not know the meaning of in a book, it causes me to pause each time I see them in the text, taking me out of the story. Here is a brief list of foreign words and meanings I have used in this book.

Bebe: Baby (Term of endearment)

Belle: Beautiful

Connard: Asshole

Crétin arrogant: Arrogant jerk

Eveque: Bishop

Fils de pute: Son of a bitch

La mien: Mine

L'amour de ma vie: Love of my life

L'enfer: hell

Ma chérie: My darling

Merde: Shit

Mon amour: My love

Non: No

Oui: Yes

Pauvre batard: Poor bastard

Plan de sauvegarde: Back-up plan

Putain: The French equivalent of saying fuck

Putain, j'adore ces bottes: Fuck, I love these boots.

Soutien-gorge: bra

Tu es à moi et seulement à moi, Belle. Pour toujours: You are mine, and only mine, beautiful. Forever.

Prologue

Paris, France

Beep. Beep. Beep.

Balls deep in the woman of his dreams, Gabriel paused.

Beep. Beep. Beep.

The woman beneath him blurred, and then disappeared altogether as his eyes fluttered open to find himself exactly as he'd gone to bed. Alone. Gabriel groaned and rolled over, seeking the red numerals of his alarm clock — 2.45 a.m. He flopped on his back, his unsatisfied cock tenting the blanket. *Putain.* He'd dreamed of her again. His mate. The woman he'd left in Paris three Christmases ago.

He scrubbed his hand across his face, trying to banish her from his thoughts. Blue eyes and a sexy smile goaded him.

Beep. Beep. Beep.

Gabriel frowned. What the hell *was* that? It wasn't loud like a car alarm, or the whoop whoop of a fire alarm, but to his sensitive hearing it might as well have been blaring from the ceiling.

Beep. Beep. Beep.

Putain. He threw back the covers. One thing was for certain—it wasn't going to stop until he figured out what it was and shut it the fuck off.

Grumbling, he dragged himself and his throbbing balls from his bed and padded out into his living area. Christmas lights winked on and off on the over-decorated Christmas tree—courtesy of his younger twin brothers—washing the room in green, red and blue. Had the flashing lights tripped an alarm? No. The annoying as fuck beeping was coming from his office.

He turned his back on the Christmas monstrosity, stalked across his living area and nudged open his office door. Numerous computer screens stared back at him as he pushed into the room. Black, silent, the only thing he saw in them was his own naked reflection. Except for one.

Beep. Beep. Beep.

A green curser flashed in time with the beeping. An alarm he'd set. For what? His fingers raced over the keyboard, calling up the data. He stilled, staring at the screen.

Fuck me.

Someone was mining the internet for information on Eveque Faucher. Someone in San Francisco, California. It was her. It had to be. The witch who would be sent back in time to target Faucher—a tenth-century witch hunter and his ancestor's arch nemesis. Sent back to prevent the slaughter of thousands of woman—witches—and change the course of history.

Bella Rodriguez. The witch. Gabriel and his brothers wouldn't be born if she didn't go. She'd stayed and mated his ancestors. She would become his paternal many times great grandmother.

Gabriel snatched up his phone, the ache in his balls momentarily forgotten. It was time for him to go to California.

Chapter One

San Francisco, California
USA

It was all Annabelle Jackson-Rodriguez could do to keep her expression neutral and not betray the turmoil raging inside her. Fury, shock and — Lord help her — desire, rolled over her hotter than the Santa Ana winds.

A flush rose up her neck and she wished she'd chosen to wear the turtleneck sweater instead of her cardigan. Her hands twitched at her side and her gaze roamed ceaselessly, lighting on objects in the room — on the imposing desk, the bookshelf filled with books on arcane knowledge, the wind-whipped San Francisco Bay beyond the floor-to-ceiling windows. The Christmas tree in the corner — the High Priestess' nod to social norms — with its red, green and gold decorations and store-wrapped presents beneath like something from the pages of a Home Beautiful Christmas Edition. The High Priestess with her coiffed hair and tailored suit designed to impress her millionaire real estate clients. Annabelle looked anywhere and everywhere but at the object of her distress. Gabriel Madore.

The High Priestess had called her in for a meeting. Her and—Annabelle leveled a sneer at the man standing next to her—Dutton King. A matter of great importance, she'd said. No witch could, or would ignore a summons from the leader of the coven. Annabelle had her suspicions as to the nature of the summons. What Dutton was doing here was anyone's guess, but Gabriel... He was the last person she'd expected to encounter. Here of all places. And he hadn't come alone.

Three years. Three long years, numerous, though short-lived—*very* short-lived—relationships, of which none had ever compared, blasted from her memory the moment she'd set eyes on Gabriel again. Standing there, beside the leader of her coven, in a snug pair of black Levi's, a torso hugging T-shirt and a curl of dark hair flopping over one brown eye. She wanted to draw back and punch him in the nose. Wipe that smirk off his lips. Cast a spell and turn him into a toad. If only.

Where had he gone? That night in Paris?

Annabelle's gaze slid to the unfamiliar woman next to him. Athletic, strong and—acid burned in the back of her throat—gorgeous. Was she why he'd left her? After two glorious, passionate months of mind-blowing sex in the city of love? Where they hadn't been able to get enough of each other. Where the fire between them had threatened to swallow them up and consumed— Annabelle dropped her gaze to her shoes. Well, it had obviously consumed only her. Otherwise, he would never have left her standing in the damn street on Christmas Eve.

"I have to go," he'd said, beneath the Christmas lights of the Champs-Élysées, regret shining in his eyes. "I'm sorry."

Then he'd handed her their parcels—chocolates, artisan cheeses and hand-crafted Christmas ornaments purchased on their stroll through the Christmas markets—and walked away. The last she'd seen of him were his broad shoulders as he'd slipped into a cab. Then he was gone.

She'd spent Christmas Day alone in her little rented apartment in the fourth arrondissement, watching lovers stroll along the Seine while she had only her memories and her thoughts of what might have been to keep her company. Christmas had always been more a time for spending with family rather than anything of religious significance for Annabelle. But after Paris, even that had lost its luster… It was hard to be festive and jolly with the memory of Gabriel and Paris rattling around in her head and her heart.

Now he was here. On her home turf. With a woman. The Christmas tree in the corner mocked her.

I hate Christmas.

She squared her shoulders and lifted her chin. She was not going to let him intimidate her. Not here. Not now. She'd moved past him.

He ran his gaze leisurely over her, from head to toe, and God help her if it didn't remind her of what it felt like to have his hands caressing her and teasing her to heights she had never reached since. She glared at him, and he openly grinned. She scowled.

"Annabelle." The High Priestess turned that impenetrable slate gaze of hers on her. "Pay attention."

"My apologies, High Priestess," she mumbled.

That the most powerful witch in their coven was her great aunt afforded Annabelle no concessions, not when it came to coven matters.

"Jeez, Annabee," whispered Dutton. "What is it with you and this guy? Another one of your jilted lovers?"

Dutton King—warlock and all-round pain in her ass. She'd forgotten he was there. She rolled her lips, smothering her laugh. He wouldn't like that. Being forgotten. With a name like King and an attitude to match, he strutted around their coven as if he ruled it. If he and his family had their way, he'd soon be one step closer. *That* wasn't happening. Never in a million years would she consider a match with him. Especially not now she'd seen him wearing that ridiculous Christmas sweater. What grown man wore *anything* with Rudolph the Red-nosed Reindeer on it?

His fingers brushed hers. Annabelle recoiled. She didn't have to turn Dutton into a toad. He already was one. She clasped her hands behind her back, out of his reach. A growl rumbled, and Annabelle's attention snapped to Gabriel. Dark eyes bored into hers and his lips curled into a snarl. She stuck out her chin.

How dare he? He'd left her without a follow-up phone call, not even a text. And now he stood there, with a woman, and he was upset because another man tried to touch her? If having anything to do with Dutton didn't make her skin crawl, she might have grabbed for his hand just to spite the gorgeous hunk of man flesh she'd once called her lover.

The High Priestess, her aunt, sighed. "Do we need to clear the air here? Before we can get down to business?"

Annabelle shook her head. "Nope. I've got nothing to say."

Dutton puffed up his chest. "Well, I do."

Annabelle rolled her eyes. *Of course he does.*

"I don't know what's gone on between you two in the past," he said, flicking his gaze between Annabelle and Gabriel, "but it's over. Annabelle is my intended and I'll not have some...some *shifter* sniffing around my woman."

Gabriel's nostrils flared.

Annabelle snorted. "*Your* woman? Only in your dreams, Dutton. Wait. *What?*" She spun on Gabriel. "You're a shifter? How did I not know that?"

Gabriel shrugged.

Annabelle wanted to wipe the smug smirk off Dutton's face. With her boot.

"This is why, Annabee, you need me," said Dutton. "Any witch or warlock with any experience would know he's a wolf shifter." He gave a sweep of his hand to include Xena: Warrior Princess. "They're both shifters." He looked down his nose at Annabelle. "You're not strong enough to rule this coven on your own, sweets. You need me."

He brushed the back of his hand across her cheek, and her stomach roiled. She pulled back, resisting the urge to gag. She stared at Gabriel and the woman beside him. The beautiful woman. The she-wolf. Is that why he'd left her? Had his pack called him back to mate one of their own?

She faced the pride and joy of the King family. "Now is not the time for this discussion, Dutton, but I assure you, you are the last man I would *ever* need."

"Enough!" Her aunt slammed a book down on her desk. "Our visitors are not here to discuss the internal politics of our coven." She glared at Annabelle before turning to Dutton. "Nor your marriage proposal, Dutton."

Marriage proposal? Oh, hell, no.

Dutton must've tired of her refusals and approached the High Priestess. Her aunt wouldn't do that, would she? Take her choice away and marry her off to Dutton for the benefit of the coven? Annabelle pulled herself together. Her aunt had said marriage *proposal*, not impending marriage.

"Gabriel Montagne and Stefanie d'Louncrais are here as representatives of the Langeais Wolf pack."

Montagne? Bastard. He'd told her his name was Gabriel Madore. It was part of the reason she'd initially thought he was Spanish, not French. That, and he looked like Zorro. Or the actor who played him.

"They've come all the way from France."

At least he hadn't lied about being French.

How did I not know what he was? Not sense he was a wolf shifter?

She bit her lip. God, it was so obvious. His size, his muscular build, his stamina in bed. The way he'd always known when she was aroused. How he'd known what turned her on and when she was ready for him. Lord, he'd anticipated everything — from her need for him, whether she was tired, excited, happy, when she was hungry. She'd thought, at the time, they'd been in tune with each other. Soul mates. *How naïve he must have thought me.*

Her gaze dropped to his wrist, to the leather cuff with the silver wolf motif he'd never taken off. She'd thought it nothing more than a decorative wristband. *She* had one, too. Stefanie. Like a badge of honor, proclaiming to the world what they were. A shifter's version of a biker's club patch on their leathers. How could she have been so blind? To not have seen what was right in front of her eyes?

"It appears," continued her aunt, "our search for historical figures who had an undeniable impact on witches over the centuries has caught their attention."

"Which search, exactly?" asked Dutton.

"One of yours, Dutton. Which is why you are here."

Dutton smirked. Annabelle's nails bit into her palms. The moron would be insufferable now.

"Eveque Faucher, to be specific."

Annabelle frowned. "Eveque Faucher?" She'd never heard of him.

Dutton shot her a pitying look. "Let me guess, Annabee. You stuck with the well-known ones. Remigius, or Martin del Rio."

Remigius was an inquisitor who'd boasted he'd burned nine hundred witches in fifteen years. Martin del Rio claimed he'd killed five hundred in Geneva in a three-month period. When the High Priestess had set them the task of finding one historical figure whose removal would significantly impact the trajectory of the witch trials, of course she'd gone for the big ones. The ones who'd killed a lot of people, witches included. Remigius, Martin del Rio and Matheus Hopkins, the Witchfinder General. At the top of her list—Heinrich Kramer and Jacob Springer, authors of *Malleus Maleficarum*, the Hammer of Witches.

"You need to brush up on your history, Annabee. Eveque Faucher, Bishop Faucher, was a tenth-century witch hunter."

"Tenth century? The persecution of witches didn't really start until the fourteenth century."

"Tsk, tsk, Annabee." Dutton sighed and shook his head. "With something this important, you need to think outside the box."

Annabelle rolled her eyes. "Don't patronize me, Dutton. And stop calling me Annabee. You know I hate it."

"Let me explain it to you so you can understand, *Annabee.*"

She gritted her teeth. Could the man be any more insufferable?

"You see—"

"Eveque Faucher was a studier of what was, in the tenth century, considered the dark arts," interrupted the woman, Stefanie.

Her voice was soft and melodious, her French accent strong, but there was steel in her green gaze. *Yay for female solidarity.*

Dutton glared at Stefanie. "As I was saying, before I was rudely interrupted, Eveque Faucher—"

"—hunted down witches, werewolves and anything of a paranormal nature," continued Stefanie, ignoring Dutton, focusing solely on Annabelle.

Annabelle glanced at Dutton. His face was red, and he looked like he was going to blow a gasket. Annabelle didn't want to like Stefanie, not if she was the reason Gabriel had ghosted her, but she had to give the woman points for putting Dutton in his place.

Dutton was all but vibrating with rage. "If you'll just let me—"

"Faucher had many supporters," said Stefanie, as though Dutton hadn't spoken at all. "One of them was an ancestor of Heinrich Kramer."

"And that, my dear Annabee," rushed in Dutton, "is why I focused on a tenth-century bishop."

"Well done, Dutton," said the High Priestess.

His frustration vaporizing with the simple praise, Dutton rocked back on his heels and grinned at her. "Thank you, High Priestess."

Supercilious bastard.

"And that brings us to why we are here," said Gabriel.

Annabelle nearly swooned at the familiarity of that deep voice. A voice that had once romanced her over dinner and a bottle of Bordeaux. Had commanded her to spread her legs for him so he could taste her, and had whispered dirty words against her throat as he'd thrust inside her. Her legs quivered, and her panties dampened.

Gabriel's nostrils flared, and his gaze locked with hers. He knew. *Damn it. Bloody shifter senses.* She dropped her gaze, willing her body to have some level of dignity. The man had clearly moved on. That her body betrayed her continuing need for him was embarrassing. Lord knew what Stefanie thought of it all.

"Tell us, High Priestess," said Gabriel. "What is your interest in Eveque Faucher?"

The High Priestess shrugged an elegant shoulder. "We plan to rewrite history."

Chapter Two

Gabriel glanced from the High Priestess to Annabelle, then to the warlock — the man who thought he had some sort of claim over Annabelle. His Annabelle. *Like hell.*

It had been three years since he'd last seen her. Three *fucking* long years with the memory of her sweet body clenching around his cock on constant replay every time he closed his damn eyes. God, he'd missed her laughter, her sass. Her cornflower-blue eyes twinkling to rival all the Christmas lights in Paris. Or hooded, with her full lips puffy from his attentions and her long blonde hair splayed across his pillow. He hadn't wanted to leave her. God, it'd been the hardest thing he'd ever done, getting into that taxi. The look on her face, the confusion, then the disbelief. That last glimpse of her, the dawning understanding in her eyes, still haunted him. He'd had no choice. His pack had needed him.

What a shock to find her here. *And* to find out she's a witch. But, as his pack knew all too well, fate often played a hand in these things. Now here he was, on pack business, nearly three years to the day since he'd left her on the Champs-Élysées, and he was damned if he was going to leave here without her. Nothing would stand in his way this time. Not his pack, not the High Priestess, and most definitely not a pretentious, overconfident warlock.

He grinned. *Merry Christmas to me.*

Gabriel turned to the High Priestess. "What exactly do you mean when you say you want to rewrite history?"

The High Priestess leaned back in her chair and regarded them. "Imagine if someone could go back in time and kill Hitler *before* he rallied the people. Or Osama Bin Laden, while he was only a boy. Or Stalin, or Pol Pot, before they became responsible for so many deaths. Would you hesitate, or would you act?"

She paused and arched a manicured eyebrow. "It's estimated somewhere between thirty-five and sixty *thousand* people, predominantly women, died during the Inquisition. Many of those people were nothing more than victims of gossip, superstition and overzealous churchmen. Some of them were genuine witches, dedicated to helping and healing those who sought their aid." Herer keen eyes studied him, watching for his reaction. "What if we could change that? What if, with one carefully orchestrated and targeted attack, we could prevent the Inquisition from ever happening?"

"Interesting proposition." Gabriel side-eyed Stef. "I'm sure many people have wondered how different the world would be if we could go back in time and change things. There's a whole genre of fiction dedicated to the idea, but no one has invented a machine that can travel through time. Yet, here you are talking as if it is a possibility."

Oh, it was possible. That he'd even been born was proof of that. Not something he was planning on sharing with Marjory Jackson.

"Oh, I assure you, Mr. Montagne, it *is* a possibility. A very *real* possibility."

Gabriel feigned surprise. "How?"

"Now, now, Mr. Montagne," she said, tapping a manicured finger on her desk. "You can hardly expect me to divulge our coven's secrets."

She smiled at him, a perfectly practiced smile that spoke of class and manners, but there was no denying this woman was a formidable opponent. Behind the façade of elegance lurked a dangerous and powerful woman. She wouldn't be single-handedly ruling her coven if she wasn't. According to his brothers, Pierre and Louis, the computer geeks of the pack, she'd been running the coven for nigh on forty years. The lines around her eyes and her gray hair might hint at her age, but this woman was no geriatric. The High Priestess, Marjory Jackson, would not roll over and give them what they wanted. He hadn't expected she would.

But the Langeais wolves weren't easy pickings, either. They might be here to ensure the witch went back in time, and to help prepare her for the tenth century, to give her knowledge of the pack and warn her of the situation she was stepping in to, but Gabriel wasn't going to lay out all their secrets for them. Not when the coven had one of their own. Like, where the hell had *they* come across a way to time travel?

Oui, the pack had sacred amulets that could traverse time. Not their original purpose, but something their ancestors had discovered possible when archeologist Erin Richardson had found one and zapped herself back to the tenth century. But the spell that had created them, and all knowledge of them, were a more closely guarded secret than their very existence. As were all remaining amulets, as far as Gabriel was aware.

Besides, there was no guarantee what year, or what century, an amulet would take a person to. Had these witches stumbled across one and found a way to target a specific time and place? Or a spell of their own, perhaps? That was one spell the Langeais wolves would love to get their hands on.

"Perhaps," said Marjory, the sweetness of her smile not matching the steeliness of her gaze, "you could share with us why our coven's internet search caught your attention."

"Of course." He had to give Marjory something, and as long as it fit with their end goal and did not compromise the pack, he was authorized to divulge certain facts. "The Langeais wolves had dealings with Eveque Faucher. Not good ones. He hunted our pack and a witch under our pack's protection. And he kept detailed descriptions of his endeavors. Our ancestors searched for those writings, hoping to find them and destroy them, but they were unsuccessful." Gabriel raked his hand through his hair. "You understand, we cannot allow such information to fall into the wrong hands. Even now, there is an element of society who wish to eradicate us. Like his writings on witchcraft, should this information come to light, it could do immeasurable damage."

Marjory Jackson inclined her perfectly coiffed head. "Well, we agree then. Targeting Eveque Faucher is advantageous to us both. Do you have information that could aid us in eliminating Faucher?"

Gabriel bit back a smile. "We do."

"And would you be willing to share that information? Work with us on a mutually beneficial plan?"

Gabriel pretended to weigh up the request. He glanced at Stef. She frowned and pursed her lips, studying the witches in the room for a moment as though considering their options, then gave a brief dip of her chin.

Gabriel nodded. "Yes. In return for our assistance…"

Marjory Jackson's raised eyebrow spoke volumes.

"…we would like to know how you plan to send someone back through time."

The woman barely blinked, masking her thoughts and her emotions. Most people's bodies would betray them, and Gabriel never had any trouble reading them. No shifter would. But Marjory Jackson gave nothing away.

The spell would have to be here. In this office. She'd want to keep it close. Same with an amulet, if she had one. The bookshelf, perhaps? That was the obvious place. Or on the Christmas tree, hidden in its faux branches. Or boxed up as a present artfully arranged at its base? Could a shiny bauble conceal an amulet within?

"I'll consider it, depending on how useful you prove to be."

Gabriel smiled. "That's all we ask." He'd break into this office every night he was here, rip that tree and every bauble on it to pieces if he had to. They would have their answer before they were done. "Now," he rubbed his hands together. "Who's the lucky witch — or warlock — you plan to send back to the tenth century?"

"Our strongest and most proficient member of our coven."

Gabriel doubted that, knowing where, and in what condition, his ancestor had found Bella Rodriguez.

Dutton beamed and his chest puffed out. "Well, thank you, High Priestess, for your confidence —"

"My niece. Annabelle."

What? Annabelle. His Annabelle. *Putain. No. She's the wrong witch. Merde.* They had their work cut out for them here.

Dutton gaped at the High Priestess. "But...but...I..." He snapped his mouth shut and glared at Annabelle.

Annabelle smirked. "Like I said before, Dutton, I don't need *you*."

Marjory turned to her niece, all business. "Annabelle Jackson-Rodriguez, do you consent to undertake this task for the benefit of your coven and all witches, past, present and future?"

Gabriel's lungs seized as he stared at Annabelle. No, it couldn't be. She was... But... *Annabelle. Jackson. Rodriguez. Bella Rodriguez.* It wasn't possible. He'd thought... With a name like Bella Rodriguez... With the olive skin and dark brown eyes his family were known for, he'd thought... Hell, they'd *all* thought the American Bella Rodriguez was Hispanic or Latino. Annabelle, *his Belle*, was blonde and blue-eyed.

Since when had her name been Rodriguez? Or Jackson? She'd told him her name was Annabelle Newman. She'd *lied* to him.

You lied to her, too.

He had, but... *Merde,* what sort of excuse for a shifter was he that he'd failed to scent her lie? He was head of pack security, for fuck's sake. But he'd been so caught up in her, in that sexy smile, in her determined independence, that he'd missed it. His nose had let him down. No wonder he hadn't been able to find her. How many months had Pierre and Louis wasted trying to track an American woman named Annabelle Newman for him? He'd never live it down if his brother's found out the truth.

Annabelle squared her shoulders and raised her chin. "Yes, High Priestess, I do. Thank you for believing in me."

"Well, then, it's settled." Marjory clapped her hands together. "Time to get to work. We have history to change."

Chapter Three

"Annabelle, wait."

Annabelle ignored Gabriel. Yes, they had to work together, but right now she needed a little fresh air. A moment to think. She was taking a trip back in time to the tenth century—*Ugh! No toilets, no coffee, no equality for women* – Dutton had bypassed her refusals and gone straight to the High Priestess requesting—no, probably demanding—her hand in marriage, and Gabriel was here, reigniting the passion she'd thought she'd laid to rest. No, not dead, just buried. And not deep enough, if the dampness of her panties and the rub of her clothes against her peaked nipples was anything to go by.

She stomped her way down the hall. *Merry fucking Christmas to me.*

"Sending a woman back to that barbaric time is a mistake," grumbled Dutton as he kept pace with her. "It should be a man. It should be—"

Annabelle stopped and spun on Dutton. "It should be you? Newsflash, dude, it's the twenty-first century. It's politically incorrect and downright misogynistic to think a woman couldn't do this job as well as, if not better than, a man. Especially when *you're* that man." She sneered up at him. "You may think you're the bee's knees, Dutton, but you're going down that road alone." She raked her gaze over his sweater to the reindeer in the center, where its red pompom nose bobbled about. "Really, Dutton? A Rudolph sweater? Could you possibly be any more of an embarrassment to the coven?"

As handsome as he was, Dutton was no Mark Darcy. Not to Annabelle. No matter what he wore. Everything about Dutton made her skin itch.

Dutton ran his hand over the woolen Rudolph. "My great aunt knitted it for me. The woman is in her eighties. There are very few pleasures left in her life. Wearing it is the least I could do."

If Dutton was trying to make her feel bad, he'd failed. His great aunt was no sweet, doddering old lady who spent her days knitting by the fireplace and giving sweets to her grandchildren any more than the High Priestess was. She was a wizened old crone who ruled the King clan with an iron fist and a wicked tongue. Her idea of pleasure was making everyone in a fifty-mile radius jump to do her bidding and raining down hellfire on them when they didn't move fast enough. If Dutton himself wasn't reason enough not marry into the King clan, Cordelia King certainly was.

Gabriel and Stefanie exited her great aunt's study. They paused, and Gabriel said something to Stefanie she couldn't hear, something that made Stefanie frown and her body stiffen. What Annabelle wouldn't give for shifter hearing right about now.

Then Stefanie retreated into the High Priestess' office and Gabriel walked toward her. *Nope.* She was not ready for that conversation. Not yet. She turned and headed for the front door, desperate to get away and to clear her head.

"I won't risk my future bride—"

Annabelle froze. Slowly, deliberately, she walked back to Dutton and glared up at him. "Future *bride?* In. Your. Dreams. Dutton. King. I will never"—Annabelle poked Rudolph in the eye and the pompom jerked wildly—"ever"—another poke, so forceful Dutton took a step back—"be. Your. Bride." It took everything she had to get the words out at a decibel that wouldn't be heard across the street. "I don't care if the High Priestess were to order me to marry you, I wouldn't. I'd rather get stuck in the tenth century, married to some barbarian marauder, than have *anything* to do with you."

A low growl rumbled behind her. Dutton paled. He might be six feet tall and spend most of his days in the gym, but he was no match for Gabriel. Montagne suited Gabriel far more than Madore. He truly lived up to the English translation of his name. At six feet four, he was a mountain of a man. As a shifter, he was lethal. Dutton going up against Gabriel would be like a chihuahua taking on a grizzly bear. But she didn't need or want Gabriel to fight for her.

"This is none of your business, Gabriel. Back off."

Dutton removed her finger from his chest. "You'll come around. Everyone can see the benefit of joining our two families. It'll make the coven stronger. We're a good match, you and I, Annabelle. With us at ruling together, there'll not be single witch or shifter that would dare challenge us. Or this coven." He grabbed hold of her chin, ignoring Annabelle's recoil. "We'd make beautiful babies, too, to follow in our footsteps. And despite what you say, even you're not willful enough to disobey a command from the High

Priestess." He glanced warily over her shoulder at Gabriel. "And set him straight. I'll not have some random hookup of yours coming between us."

With that, he turned on his heel and stormed off down the hall, the slam of the front door behind him echoing through the house. Annabelle snorted. *Dutton has left the building. Arrogant ass.*

She spun on Gabriel and folded her arms across her chest. *One down, one more to go.*

Gabriel mirrored her stance, his biceps flexing.

Don't drool, don't drool.

"We need to talk."

Annabelle scoffed. "Talk? It's a shame you didn't want to *talk* in Paris. You know, before you disappeared into the crowd of last-minute Christmas shoppers."

"I had no choice, Belle."

"Yeah, whatever. Did you know?"

He frowned. "Know what?"

"That I was a witch."

They both turned as a maid entered the hall, a vacuum cleaner in tow. Gabriel grabbed her arm and tugged her into the downstairs bathroom, closed the door and flicked the lock behind them.

Ignoring the prickle of goosebumps at his touch, Annabelle wrenched her arm free. "Did you know I was a witch when we were in Paris?"

Gabriel shook his head. "No. I wish I had. It may have changed things."

"Like you might have told me your real name?"

"Like you told me yours?"

Annabelle had forgotten about that. There'd been trouble amongst the covens, and with some of the shifter clans. It'd been a real mess, and she'd craved anonymity, nothing connecting her to her coven or witchcraft. Just for a few months. It was part of the reason she'd gone to Paris, and why she'd given Gabriel a fake surname. It still didn't excuse him for ditching her like an unwanted Christmas gift. On Christmas Eve, no less.

She dragged in a deep breath, needing to know yet not really wanting to. "Why did you leave?"

Gabriel looked away. "Belle…" His sigh was full of regret.

"Right." She dropped her gaze and held up her hand, stopping him from giving her some lame excuse. "I get it." She forced a smile to her lips. "I was good enough for a fling, but nothing more. That's why you left, isn't it? You were called back to mate one of your own kind." She jerked her head to the door, to the hall, where no doubt his shifter mate — his gorgeous shifter mate — waited. "To mate Stefanie."

"*What*? No. Stef and I aren't… Annabelle, look at me."

When she didn't comply, when the pattern in the floor tiles continued to hold her attention, he pressed a finger beneath her chin, forcing her to look at him.

"Annabelle, I did return to my pack. They called me in, and I had no choice but to go. I couldn't tell you why. I still can't, but I can tell you it wasn't to mate a she-wolf. And I didn't want to leave you. If I'd had any other option, I would have taken it."

She rolled her eyes. *My eyeballs sure are getting a workout today.*

He cupped her chin in both hands. "Belle."

The way her name rolled off his tongue, Belle, with that French accent of his… His pet name for her. Belle — in French, it meant beautiful. She tried to shut down her body's response to him, but her skin heated and her heart pounded. He'd have to know. His shifter senses wouldn't miss it. Nor the way her body swayed, no matter how infinitesimally, toward him, drawn there like metal to a magnet.

Their gazes locked, and her breath quickened. He leaned in, hesitating mere inches from her, their breaths mingling. Her mouth suddenly as dry as the Mojave Desert, she licked her lips. With a groan, he bridged the gap.

Oh, Lordy…

Three years, and she had not forgotten the taste of him, the feel of him, nor the way his kisses set her on fire, stirring up long-denied emotions and memories of nights in his arms impossible to resist.

His tongue swiped the seam of her lips, and she parted them on a sigh. A deep rumble reverberated in his chest and the mental restraints that held her in place snapped, unable to contain the longing and the need that exploded in her chest. She flung her arms around his neck and pressed herself into him, feeling every hard plane, every muscle in his toned body and the evidence of his arousal poking her in the stomach. Lord, she'd missed this. Missed him.

He walked her backward until she hit the vanity, and he ground himself against her as his tongue plundered her mouth. How could she still want him after the way he'd left her? Lied to her? But she did. Oh God, she did. She rolled her hips, meeting his, hungry for his hot, hard cock.

With firm hands on her waist, he lifted her onto the vanity, spread her thighs and stepped between them. He broke away from her mouth to trail kisses down her throat. The scratch of his stubble, the moist flick of his tongue, those full lips — they undid her. They always had.

"God, Belle, I've been going crazy without you," he whispered, his hot breath sending goosebumps across her skin.

She should stop him. They were in the High Priestess' bathroom, for God's sake.

Annabelle tilted her head and gave him greater access. *I've missed you, too.*

He tugged at the buttons on her cardigan, parting it. Confident, he didn't tease or hesitate. Pushing the band of her bra up over her breasts, he cupped them with his large hands. Hands that knew what she liked, reminding her of what she'd been missing. He gave them a gentle squeeze and rubbed his thumb across her turgid nipple. She shuddered, her core clenching on air and her thighs quivering against his sides.

"Belle."

He dropped his head and sucked her nipple into his mouth. Heat shot straight to her clit and damn, she almost came. This. This is what she'd been searching for with every man who'd had the misfortune to grace her bed after Gabriel. None had ever come close to the way he could bring her body alive and have her panting for him with barely a few touches. A kiss. A swirl of tongue around her nipple, a scrape of teeth, a slide of a hand along the sensitive underside of her breast, the heady aroma of his aftershave.

God, she was so close. He released her nipple, and cool air raced across her damp skin. She wrapped her legs around him and the inseam of her jeans met his rock-hard erection, and she moaned.

"You like that, Belle?"

Gabriel pulled her in tight, pressing her swollen bare breasts against his chest, the friction of his T-shirt against them exquisite. He ground into the V of her thighs, and her legs clenched tighter. He chuckled, low and dark, and rolled his hips again. And again, and again, setting up a steady rhythm. She clung to him, her body lost. No longer caring he'd left her. Or that he'd most likely leave her again. Right here, right now, in the downstairs bathroom of the High Priestess' house, all she cared about was the pulsing heat between her legs desperate to be quenched.

His hot breath whispered over her lips. "Come for me, Belle."

He gave one last grind of his hips, and her mouth dropped open in a silent scream. She exploded, her heels digging into his butt and her back arched. She rode the waves, her body quivering until spent, and she collapsed against him, her chest heaving. No other man had ever played her body as well as Gabriel. Neither before nor after.

The hardness of the vanity, and the unpleasant sensation of the brushed gold tapware digging into her hip, pulled her from her post-orgasmic stupor.

Annabelle released Gabriel and covered her face with her hands.

What the hell have I just done?

Chapter Four

Every cell in Gabriel's body was attuned to the woman in his arms. His enhanced senses, his wolf and his hard-as-granite cock. *Oui*, it wanted in. He wanted to rip off her clothes, stretch her naked body out on the cold tiles and devour her. He wanted to sink into her wet heat, fuck her seven ways to Sunday until she forgave him. Until she told him she was his in every way. But as the pleasure from her orgasm faded, so, too, did Annabelle's willingness to remain in his arms.

Her legs unclenched from around his hips, and she pushed against his chest, squirming in his hold. "Let me go."

As much as his wolf rebelled, he did as she asked, stepping back and allowing her to slip off the vanity.

"Annabelle—"

"Don't."

She readjusted her *soutien-gorge*—a delicate pink lace that cupped her beautiful breasts to perfection and made him want to sink his face between those glorious, creamy mounds.

"This…" She wouldn't look at him as she buttoned up her cardigan. "It was a mistake. It shouldn't have happened." Her face was flushed, and her eyes were bright, but she pressed her lips into a thin line and tilted her chin up at him. "We have a job to do, and it doesn't involve you fucking me and leaving again."

She pushed past him, flicking the lock and opening the door. "Call the High Priestess when you're ready to get down to actual business. Until then, I've got work to do."

He reached for her, but she slipped out of the bathroom and slammed the door in his face.

He raked a hand through his hair. "Well, that went better than I expected."

His cock didn't agree. It pressed up against his zipper, throbbing in tandem with his balls. He took a deep breath, willing it to calm down. He couldn't very well step out into the hall and front up to the High Priestess with a raging erection.

The door to the bathroom swung open and Stef leaned against the door frame, her arms folded across her chest. "Tell me you didn't just do what I think you did?"

He rubbed his hand across his chin. "Nope."

"Oh, please. I can smell her on you, and I could hear you."

"I didn't fuck her, Stef. I wanted to, and she wanted me to, no matter what she might say, but I didn't." He clocked her skeptical expression, and waved his hand in front of his groin. "You think I'd still be in this condition if I had?"

Stef blew out a breath. "So, want to fill me in? Before this becomes a complete mess and the High Priestess sends us packing."

"Annabelle and I have history."

Stef chortled. "Big surprise there." She tilted her head and regarded him with those piercing green eyes of hers. "This must be difficult for you, finding out you've slept with your ancestor."

He shook his head. "She's not. She can't be. Look at her, Stef. She's blonde and…and…*Caucasian*."

Stef shrugged. "We wouldn't be the first to make assumptions based on racial stereotypes. There could be any number of explanations for your features. One of your more recent ancestors may have been Spanish. Any one of them in the last thousand years, really, when you think about it."

"That's possible, I suppose, but…"

"Bella Rodriguez. Annabelle Jackson-*Rodriguez*. It seems pretty conclusive to me." She slapped him on the shoulder with the back of her hand. "Come on, Gabriel. We're werewolves. More than most, we should know better than to judge someone by their appearance."

Gabriel pinched the bridge of his nose. "*Oui.* I know, but… She can't be my tenth-century ancestors' mate. Edmond and Aubert can't have her."

"Why not?"

"Because she's *mine*."

Stef pushed off from the door frame. "Are you sure?"

Was he sure? Yes. He recognized the signs. The way he growled at Dutton when the warlock had staked his claim. Even in Paris, he'd known. When he'd touched her, and his body had shot to attention in a heartbeat. The way his cock no longer responded to any other woman but her, no matter how often he'd tried. He'd given up in the end and, *putain*, he was tired of using his own hand. Three long years of celibacy had sucked. If that didn't tell him she was his mate... "*Oui.*"

"Well then, this is going to be interesting."

"*Oui.*" He adjusted himself in his jeans. "Can you liaise with the High Priestess? We need to set up a meeting with Annabelle, and at least appear to be coaching her for her trip back in time. See if you can find out anything about other coven members. Maybe suggest we need a standby, a back-up plan, should something happen to Annabelle. With any luck, she'll suggest the right Bella and not that *connard*, Dutton."

She shrugged. "Okay, but you know, if there *is* no other Bella, she has to go. If she doesn't, you won't exist."

"There has to be another Bella." He pulled out his phone, searched his contacts and hit dial when he found the one he was looking for. "I'll see if Pierre and Louis have finished their deep dive into the coven. Maybe they'll have something."

"Good luck." Stef retreated to the High Priestess' office.

There *had* to be another Bella. All the Montagnes in a long line of Montagnes had dark hair, dark eyes and olive skin. They'd believed they'd gotten it from Bella Rodriguez. Racial stereotypes aside, with a name like that, what they knew about her, and their appearance, it wasn't a big leap to assume she was Hispanic or Latino. Had they got it wrong?

Stef was right. It could have come from any ancestor between then and now. Knowing of Bella, they'd looked no deeper into the Montagne family tree. *Putain.* What if the woman he knew as Annabelle Newman, blonde-haired and blue-eyed, *was* the woman who was supposed to go back in time? His gut clenched and a hand fisted around his heart.

No. She's mine. I'm sure of it.

Merde. Why the hell couldn't his ancestors have been more like Stef's? It was the d'Louncrais journal that had warned them about Erin Richardson, the archaeologist who disappeared on a dig site in Langeais in 2016, only to turn up in the tenth century as the mate of Gaharet d'Louncrais. Apparently, Stef had inherited her green eyes. Next had come Rebekah Clarke, a bartender from London who'd disappeared one rainy night in two thousand and twenty-two. She'd mated Ulrik Voclain.

Then there was Bella Rodriguez—a witch from the United States. She'd traveled back to the tenth century some time in 2024 and mated his ancestors, twins Edmond and Aubert Montagne. Though the journal had mentioned Rebekah and Bella, the only one with any detail, any description, had been Erin.

The ringing stopped, and the phone clicked. *Finally.*

"Pierre—"

"Je ne suis pas en mesure de répondre a votre appel pour le moment. Veuillez laisser un message et je vous repondrai des que possible."

"Putain." His voicemail.

He selected another number and tried again. Same answer. This time from Louis.

Gabriel hit end and checked his watch—five p.m. That made it...one a.m. in France. Pierre and Louis were either sleeping or partying. Or, knowing his younger brothers, they had a party for three going on. He snorted. What was it with the twins in their family? Like his tenth-century ancestors, Edmond and Aubert, his brothers preferred to share. He shoved his phone back into his pocket. He'd get nothing from them for a few hours.

Gabriel retraced his steps back to the High Priestess' office. Stef was right. If Annabelle was the Bella Rodriguez the journal talked about, he'd have to let her go. If he didn't, he wouldn't exist. His whole life, everything, gone in the blink of an eye as if he had never been born at all. But letting her go… He'd walked away from her once, in Paris, and it was the hardest thing he'd ever done in his life. To let her go again might very well destroy him.

Chapter Five

Annabelle dropped her bag to the floor, slammed her apartment door behind her, and leaned up against it. What the hell had she done? Resisting Gabriel was going to be so much harder now she'd had a reminder of how explosive it was between the two of them. In the intervening years since Paris, she'd single-mindedly worked on erasing the feel of his hands on her body, his kisses, his musky scent and the way she came undone in his arms. She'd thought she'd succeeded, but one look at him in the High Priestess' office, one swipe of his tongue against hers and one grind of his hips pressing his thick length against her core, and she was back in Paris where they'd spent more time having sex than eating. And they'd spent a lot of time eating.

She let her head thump back against the door. *Damn my stupid body. And damn him.* Why, of all the Langeais shifters, did it have to be him they'd sent?

Isobella, her flatmate and stepsister, poked her head into the hall. "Are you okay?"

Annabelle groaned. *Am I okay?* She was going to have to be.

"What did the High Priestess want?" Isobella folded her arms across her chest, a defensive measure Annabelle recognized.

Though Isobella showed remarkable promise with her magic, her family had not been prominent in their coven. Not until Isobella's father had married Annabelle's mother a few years ago. Being married into the Jackson family had elevated their status right to the top. But years of conditioning was hard to undo, and the whispers through the coven were hard to ignore. So it was always High Priestess, and never Aunt Marjory, with Isobella.

To be fair, it wasn't all in Isobella's head. Coven politics could be brutal. Some families were always vying for control, like the Kings and their cronies, and they'd seen the marriage as a grab for power by the Rodriguez family. Not even Annabelle and her mother taking on the Rodriguez name had managed to quash that. Annabelle couldn't care less what the Kings thought. But Isobella did. Annabelle had changed her name for her.

Annabelle pushed herself off the door. "I have a new task."

"To do with all that research you've been doing?"

Annabelle nodded. "Yeah."

Wariness descended over Isobella's features. "She wants you to be the one to go back in time, doesn't she?"

Annabelle picked up her bag. "Would you rather it be Dutton? Because he wanted it to be him."

Isobella screwed up her nose.

"My thoughts exactly. Don't worry, Isobella," she said, patting her sister on the shoulder. "I'll be fine. We've got two wolf shifters from France who" — she hooked two fingers in the air like imaginary quotation marks — "apparently have knowledge of the time I'm to go back to. I wanted to be the one to take on this task. I just didn't expect I'd be going as far back as the tenth century."

"The *tenth* century?"

Isobella's unease matched her own. The mission was always going to be dangerous. Being a witch in medieval Europe wasn't an enviable position. Being a twenty-first century witch in medieval Europe meant there were so many more ways she could make a mistake and become one of the accused, one of thousands of women who'd died. But the tenth century was an unknown quantity. No witch trials. That was a bonus. But what *would* she be facing? A plague? Wars? She hadn't done any research that far back, and didn't have a clue what to expect? Could she trust Gabriel to prepare her for it? And why were he and Stefanie really here? Sure, their pack had a connection to this bishop — and not in a good way — but was there more to it than that? What was it they weren't telling them?

Maybe someone else should go, someone with no history with the enigmatic shifter, but they weren't flush with choices. Dutton was the obvious one, but there was no way her aunt would give Dutton an opportunity like this. Not if she didn't want to give his family any more influence within the coven than they already had. There was Douglas, but recent events would sway the decision against him. That Isobella now lived with Annabelle, that Douglas had dumped her in favor of his bit on the side — a witch from the

King family — said everything. Her aunt would always back her family, including those added to it through marriage. And there was not a chance in hell they'd trust anyone with a connection to the King family, no matter how fleeting it might be.

Dutton and Douglas. Two dickheads with a capital D.

There were a few other witches, one or two warlocks, but their loyalties were untested. No. She was the best person to go.

Annabelle followed Isobella into the living area, the scent of pine and fresh earth hitting her. She froze in the doorway. "What's all this?"

She knew what it was. She just couldn't believe it was in her apartment. In the corner, by the window, sat a Christmas tree in a pot, a length of red tinsel winding around it and clinging to its needles. Boxes of unopened ornaments in bright colors littered the floor.

Isobella shrugged. "I know. It's weird for witches to celebrate Christmas, but it was something my mother always did. She liked the decorations, the spirit of family get-togethers." Isobella held up a shoebox with the word Paris scrawled across it in black marker. "And I found these behind some towels in the linen closet." "I figured your family was the same, too. I mean, the High Priestess has a tree in her office…"

Her voice trailed off as Annabelle stared transfixed at the box in Isobella's hands. Too beautiful to throw out, and yet too painful to look at, she'd packed the delicate, hand-carved Christmas ornaments she'd bought with Gabriel in an old shoe box and shoved them to the back of the linen closet. There they'd sat for three years, undisturbed, but never forgotten. She'd never had a Christmas tree in her entire life. Not until

Christmas in Paris. Not until Gabriel. She'd gotten caught up in the festivity of it all. The snow, the lights and trawling the Christmas markets with Gabriel by her side. Then he'd left her, and she'd never had one since.

"Annabelle? I just thought... Douglas always humored me and got me a Christmas tree, and when I found these ornaments, I guess I thought..."

Annabelle shook herself and pasted a smile on her face. "Nice tree. Thanks. At least the neighbors will think we're normal, now. I'm going to have a shower." She needed to wash away the feel of Gabriel's hands and mouth on her body. Maybe then she could get back some of her equilibrium. Enough so she could face seeing a Christmas tree in her living room. So her heart wouldn't break all over again every time she glimpsed one of those ornaments. "I can't be stuffed cooking tonight. Let's order pizza, hey?"

"Sure." Isobella gave her a wan smile, and not for the first time Annabelle considered coming up with a spell to give Douglas weeping sores on his dick. See if Irena King liked him so much then. At the very least, it might make her think twice about stealing someone else's fiancée. As far as Annabelle was concerned, Douglas and Irena deserved each other.

Annabelle grabbed her backpack and headed for her room. Let Isobella have her Christmas tree. Annabelle would deal with it. A couple of to-die-for pizzas from Lenni's on the corner, a few glasses of wine and an action flick would get both her and Isobella's minds off their douchebag exes. The last thing Isobella needed was to dwell on losing Douglas. The guy wasn't worth it.

* * * *

Annabelle stepped under the shower, letting the hot water sluice over her body. She might wash away his scent and the evidence of her orgasm, but nothing was going to banish the craving, the unquenchable need he'd reignited in her. She soaped lavender body wash over breasts and her nipples hardened, desperate for any touch. Annabelle paused, then slipped her hand over her stomach. Lower still, until her fingers were sliding through her folds. She shivered and braced herself against the shower screen. Her questing fingers found her aching clit, swollen and sensitive. She flicked across it, swirled her finger around it. Annabelle closed her eyes and clenched her bottom lip between her teeth.

That's it, Belle, pleasure yourself for me. Show me how you like it.

Goosebumps prickled along her arms. Even in her head, as nothing more than a memory, Gabriel's voice had power over her body. Her hand sped up, pressing harder as she imagined it was his hand, his fingers. She slipped one inside herself, dropping her head with a muffled moan as her pussy gripped it tight. If only it was his finger, or better yet, his cock.

So wet for me, bebe.

Gabriel smiled. That sexy smile he did when he had her just where he wanted her, when he knew she was close.

I'm going to spin you around and fill you with my cock.

Annabelle quivered. So close.

I'm going to bend you over and fuck you hard.

In her mind's eye, he slid his cock inside her, filling her, sliding in and out. In and out. Eyes squeezed shut, her hand rubbing at her clit furiously, she envisioned his hard, muscled body slick with soap, pumping her from behind. Her lungs seized and her orgasm rocketed through her, and she arched her back and clamped her jaw closed, lest she scream louder than a rabid fan at the Super Bowl.

She collapsed against the shower screen and pressed her hot cheek against the wet glass. "I need to get that man out of my head."

Focus on the mission.

Yes, that's what she would do. Focus on the mission, the spell, and the work. Ignore the man. With her legs quivering and her breath uneven, Annabelle turned off the water and stepped out of the shower. There was a pizza calling with her name on it.

She dried herself off, wrapped her wet hair in a towel, turban style, and padded into her bedroom. Searching her drawer for a clean pair of panties, her fingers brushed against the item she'd buried at the back. With a glance at the door, she grabbed a pair of cotton gloves and pulled the bundle out.

Wrapped in layers of protective paper was a book. Old and fragile, the vellum pages worn and well used and tied together with strips of leather, it weighed heavy in her hands and on her soul. One look at it when her boss at Rarity—the rare and antique bookshop where Annabelle worked—had set it aside for assessment, she'd known what it was. A grimoire. A book of spells.

Ancient spells? Maybe, maybe not. Its pages *were* vellum. The bindings and the cover *were* of a medieval style. The writing *looked* like it had been done with ink and quill. But every word written was in English. *Modern* English. Not Anglo Saxon. Not Latin.

All the same, a careful, surreptitious peek at a few pages was all Annabelle had needed to determine she couldn't let this book out of her sight. Or let it fall into the wrong hands. Not these spells. Blood magic was powerful magic. It's what made Annabelle's coven so strong. Like any magic used with ill intent, the consequences could be devastating. This grimoire was full of blood magic spells, many of them meant to harm, not heal. It had taken Annabelle a split second to decide she'd have to steal the book, two days to plan her theft, and a week of waiting until her boss left for another auction in New York, before she could enact her plan. Now the grimoire sat hidden amongst her underwear.

Annabelle set it on the top of her dresser and lifted the cover, avoiding the ominous splotches of dark brownish-red. How many people had suffered at the hands of this witch?

The night she'd brought it home, after she was sure Isobella was asleep, Annabelle had read the grimoire from cover to cover. With each page, the oily sensation in her stomach had grown. This had been a dark witch, indeed.

The most benign of the spells was one at the back of the book. She turned the pages until she was staring at it. A spell to transport a person to the destination of their choice, in the present or the past. Annabelle had wondered at its inclusion. It had seemed harmless enough. Though with what her coven planned to do with it, maybe it wasn't so harmless after all. Who had used this spell in the past? And to do what?

Annabelle's first instinct had been to take the book to her great aunt, the High Priestess. Then the Kings had come sniffing around, talking of alliances between the two families, hinting Annabelle wouldn't have the support of the coven if she were to take on leadership of the coven when Aunt Marjory stepped down. Something she'd been thinking about for a while now.

The Kings had made a few insinuations, called in allegiances and stirred up old rivalries. The support for her family was waning. The idea Annabelle was strong enough to rule as High Priestess alone, as her great aunt had for the last forty years, they openly dismissed and mocked.

If the Kings were to get hold of this book, if Cordelia were to get her hands on it, there was no doubt in Annabelle's mind they would use it. Perhaps to take over the coven. If, however, the Jacksons could use it to secure their position, without doing any harm, or perhaps doing some good...

Annabelle had risked sending a photo of the time travel spell to her great aunt. She'd lied to her, the High Priestess, telling her it was a single page she'd found stuffed in the back of an illuminated manuscript from a monastery in France. Gabriel's and Stefanie's recent arrival was an unexpected boon, lending credence to her story.

They'd tested the spell, of course. Simple tests at first. Changing rooms, changing houses, always in the present. Two weeks ago, at her aunt's direction, Annabelle had used the spell to go back in time. A few weeks only. They'd taken care Annabelle would not meet herself in the past. Whether the time paradox actually existed, neither Annabelle nor her aunt cared to find out. She'd also been under strict instructions not to change anything.

The trial had been a moderate success. Annabelle had chosen the moment the grimoire had arrived at Rarity. Who knew what other books the seller might have in his possession. Unfortunately, she'd missed him by an hour. When she'd returned, she'd missed her target by several hours. The spell, it seemed, wasn't completely infallible. Would it be less accurate the greater span of time you wanted to cross? That was something they had yet to test.

A ding from her phone snapped her attention away from the spell. She quickly re-wrapped the book in its protective paper, shoved it back under her panties and bras, and dug through her bag for her phone. A text from the High Priestess.

I've arranged for you to meet Gabriel and Stefanie for dinner to discuss our plans. You have a reservation at The Lounge at the Ritz-Carlton at 7pm.

Shit. Face Gabriel again so soon? At least she wouldn't be alone. They'd be in a public place, and he was unlikely to follow her into the bathroom at the Ritz-Carlton. And Dutton wouldn't be there. *Bonus.*

She sighed. There was no help for it. If she wanted this mission, she had to go. She had no choice but to deal with Gabriel.

Wrapped in a towel, she padded out to the living room. Isobella sat on the couch absently flicking through the TV channels, the half-decorated Christmas tree abandoned. Did she seem paler than usual? More…defeated?

Despite the similarities in their names, Isobella was the yin to Annabelle's yang. Where she was fair-haired and blue-eyed, Isobella was all Latino, with long dark hair, dark eyes and that beautiful skin Annabelle had always admired. Where Annabelle was in-your-face outspoken and adventurous, Isobella was more introverted and softly spoken. But Isobella's life hadn't been easy, and there was a thread of steel beneath her quiet exterior that few people ever saw. Annabelle had thought she'd been bouncing back, smiling more. Taking a leaf out of Annabelle's play book, speaking up for herself more and demanding the respect and consideration she deserved. Maybe not.

"Hey."

Isobella looked up at her from her random scrolling.

"Just got a text from Aunt Marjory. Pizza is off the menu for me tonight. Sorry. I have a meeting at the Ritz-Carlton with our wolf shifters."

The sag of Isobella's shoulders tugged at Annabelle. Maybe she should call and cancel tonight. "Are you okay?"

Isobella shrugged. "Just a little tired." Her gaze flicked to the Christmas tree, and she sank further into the couch.

Fucking Douglas. Sometimes men were more trouble than they were worth. "I can cancel. Make it tomorrow night. The tenth century isn't going anywhere."

"And miss out on a fancy dinner at the Ritz-Carlton? You should go."

"I don't know…"

Isobella waved her off. "Cheese toasties and an early night suit me fine. I'll finish this" — she jabbed her thumb at the mess of Christmas ornaments — "and I know you're not a huge *Die Hard* fan, so I'll watch that tonight. It's the only Christmas movie I think I can stomach right now. Douglas hated it. I think he was jealous of my crush on Bruce Willis."

"If you're sure…"

"Honestly, I'll probably fall asleep halfway through the movie. Go. Enjoy."

Annabelle wasn't sure about enjoying it, but Isobella wasn't wrong about fancy. The Ritz-Carlton. Annabelle was going to order the most expensive damn thing on the menu. Gabriel would pay for ditching her, one way or another.

Chapter Six

Annabelle navigated the lobby of the Ritz-Carlton, nerves fluttering in her stomach. Her heels clicked across the floor as she passed the marble columns and walked beneath the ornate chandelier and past the faux-gold candelabras. She skirted the stunning Christmas tree, decorated in gold and silver, that almost touched the towering roof. Aunt Marjory had once tried to broker a deal to sell the penthouse here. The deal had fallen through, but given her aunt's clients wouldn't have been interested in anything under four million, it would have gone for a hefty price. Were Gabriel and Stefanie actually staying here, or did they want the coven to think they were?

She'd never found out where Gabriel had stayed in Paris. Something she'd only realized after he'd gone. For all she knew, he could be a millionaire or a beggar. He'd said he worked in security, but as he'd given her a false name, was that true or another lie? She hadn't even known he was a shifter. Did she know the man at all?

Obviously not.

Annabelle took a deep, steadying breath, squared her shoulders and, with purpose in her step, made her way to The Lounge. She'd spent too much time, and too much emotional energy, boxing up Gabriel and shoving him firmly to the back of her linen closet with the Christmas ornaments to let him back into her life now. No matter how good that orgasm in her great aunt's downstairs bathroom had been.

The maître d' smiled at her as he took her coat and scarf, and she smoothed her hands down the soft fabric of her dress. She'd dressed to kill — a woolen midnight blue sheath dress that hugged her figure, contrasted nicely with her hair and made her eyes pop. She'd paired it with heeled knee-high leather boots that not only made her look taller than her five feet seven, but accentuated the swing of her hips as she walked. Gabriel would see what he'd let go, perhaps regret it, and then Annabelle would have the victory of turning *him* down. Of walking away from *him*. She *would* walk away from him. Even if it meant she had to go to the damn tenth century to do it.

She shoved down the memories of another dinner, of another restaurant adorned to celebrate the festive season, as the maître d' led her across plush carpet, past elegant wingback chairs, to a cozy corner by the windows overlooking the San Francisco city lights. But when she set eyes on the table, her steps faltered. There was only one person waiting for her. Gabriel. Was Stefanie in the ladies' room? No. The table had only two chairs, and two place settings.

Gabriel stood. She swallowed. Blinked. A black, buttoned shirt fit snugly across his broad shoulders, and black pants hugged his hips and muscular thighs.

He looked divine in black. *Who am I kidding?* The man would look like a god in a hessian sack.

"Gabriel." Annabelle gritted her teeth, plastered a smile on her face and slid into the chair the maître d' had pulled out for her.

"Annabelle."

A server appeared with a bottle of wine. A Bordeaux. He'd remembered. She'd developed a taste for it in Paris, cultivated by him. She glanced at the label. *Château Talbot, St. Julien 1996.* Probably not the most expensive wine on the list, but it would set him back at least a couple of hundred dollars. Would it be crass to scull a whole glass of it? She fidgeted in her seat. She needed something to bolster her courage.

With the wine uncorked and tasted, and a nod of approval from Gabriel, the server poured two glasses. Annabelle snatched hers up, tempering herself and taking a sip. Flavor burst on her tongue, velvety smooth, and before she could stop it a moan slipped out. It'd been a long time since she'd enjoyed a wine this good. Over the rim of her glass, she caught the heat in Gabriel's eyes.

Annabelle set her glass down with studied calm. "Where's Stefanie? Should we be discussing our plans without her?"

Gabriel took a sip of his wine, his hand, his capable hand, cradling the wine glass. Once they had cradled… She shook her head, banishing the image that came to mind. Paris was over, in the past and it damn well had to stay there.

"By that measure, where is your great aunt?"

Of course he knew of her relationship with the High Priestess. No shifter would barge into coven business without doing a background check.

"The High Priestess cannot be everywhere or do everything all at once. In this instance, I speak for her."

"As I speak for Stef."

Damn it. Damn *him*.

"Why are you really here, Gabriel? The risk of discovery is a part of life for anyone of the supernatural variety. Taking out Faucher won't change that."

Gabriel shrugged a muscled shoulder, his shirt pulling tight across his chest. Her fingers curled. Muscle memory was a *bitch*.

"As I said earlier, in your great aunt's office, our pack has had dealings with Eveque Faucher. The information he kept on our pack, has provided — and we suspect — is still providing, our enemies with insight we wish they didn't have. If we can eliminate him and his writings, it will be of considerable benefit to us."

Lord, listening to Gabriel talk, his deep voice and that almost guttural 'r', the melodic singsong quality, even when he spoke in English... Coupled with those chocolate brown eyes, and full lips... Her nipples peaked and she squeezed her thighs together.

Gabriel swallowed, his Adam's apple bobbing. "Annabelle?"

His voice dipped deeper, huskier, and she all but melted into her panties. He reached for her hand, and she snatched it away.

"That makes sense." Did she sound a little breathy? She cleared her throat. "But you had no way of knowing we had something that could help you with that when Dutton's research alerted you to our interest in him."

"*Non.*" Gabriel tapped the table. "But what if we are wrong? What if our enemies have yet to discover Faucher's writings? Or, they have only some of them and are looking for more? Anybody, *ma chérie*, who takes an interest in Faucher is of interest to us."

Ma chérie. Literal translation, my darling. A common enough phrase in French. Gabriel had called her that many a time. In Paris. Then he'd left her. She shouldn't read anything into it.

Gabriel leaned his elbows on the table, and a whiff of his spicy aftershave mingled with the musky scent that was all Gabriel tickled her nostrils. She leaned back in her chair, resisting the urge to breathe it in, to let it surround her. Too many memories clung to that scent. Memories that stirred up a heat she was desperately trying to ignore.

"Where did the coven find the spell, Annabelle?"

Annabelle stiffened. "Who said it was a spell?"

Gabriel shrugged. "You're witches. A coven of witches. It stands to reason you would use a spell. Where did you find it?"

Why was it so important to know where it had come from? Did he suspect it was from Faucher's writings? That would mean the grimoire had belonged to the bishop. Not likely. Not unless the bishop was a warlock himself, and a dark one at that.

"Or did you write the spell, Annabelle?" he persisted. "Another witch in your coven perhaps? Or that…*warlock*, Dutton?" From the snarl in his tone as he spoke Dutton's name, it was clear what Gabriel thought of him. On this they were on the same page.

"Huh?" She shook her head. "No." She might have wished she'd written it, or that someone in her coven had — with the exception of Dutton — but no. The witch who had, had been far more proficient than she. The spell was a complicated one. Each time Annabelle had used it, she'd had to take a few hours to prepare herself for it. Transversing time was no simple matter. If it was, scientists would have discovered a way to master it by now.

Gabriel tapped the table, waiting for her reply.

"I work at Rarity. We specialize in rare and collectible books. I found it in the back of an old book." Not entirely untrue.

"And where is this book now?"

Annabelle shrugged. "Where most books in Rarity go, eventually. It got sold. As most books do sooner or later. Bought by some anonymous financier upstate, I think. I barely had a chance to take a photo of the spell before it was gone." Was he buying her lie? Her great aunt had, but a shifter's senses were far superior to a human's. "It was one page in the back of a manuscript. I had the photo, so I didn't bother tracking the sale."

His gaze slid to her purse.

"I've deleted the photo, if that's what you're looking for. It's not the kind of thing you want to leave lying around for anybody to have access to."

Did he really think she would be stupid enough to keep it on her phone? With the tech available to hackers these days? It was far too dangerous to leave it sitting in her image gallery. She'd deleted it from her phone as soon as she'd left Aunt Marjory's office. Once she'd confirmed her aunt had received it. Gabriel's gaze slid past her shoulder, then narrowed. Annabelle turned.

What the…

Strutting across the restaurant toward them was Dutton, with the maître d', red-faced and flustered, trailing along behind him.

She scowled. "Did you…?"

A snarl curled Gabriel's lips. Nope. He hadn't invited Dutton. Aunt Marjory, maybe?

"Annabee, darling. Dinner with another man? This will have to stop once we confirm our engagement."

Annabelle gripped the table. If she didn't do something with her hands, she was liable to plant her fist right into Dutton's conceited, irritating face.

Dutton stood over the shifter, his hands on his hips, and looked down his nose at him. "Gabriel."

Annabelle sighed. Was the man an idiot? Did he really think such blatant stand over tactics would work?

Gabriel merely raised an eyebrow at Dutton. "What an unpleasant surprise. I don't recall inviting you. Annabelle?"

Annabelle shook her head. "Me neither."

"As if *I* would be left out of such an important meeting." He signaled to the maître d'. "Another place setting for this table, and bring me a whiskey, neat."

Gabriel grimaced, but he gave the maître d' approval and the man hurried off.

Annabelle scowled. Aunt Marjory had better not have invited Dutton.

She pushed her chair back. "Excuse me, gentleman. I need to use the ladies' room." She slid from her seat, and because she knew it would annoy Dutton, she gave Gabriel her brightest smile and said, "Order for me, will you, *mon amour*? You know what I like."

The 'my love' was purely to piss off Dutton, but the satisfaction in Gabriel's eyes had her scurrying away and making a beeline for the ladies' room.

The door had barely closed behind her when she pulled out her phone and stabbed out an urgent text to Aunt Marjory, demanding an explanation. She paced, her heels clicking an impatient staccato on the floor.

Her phone dinged. A reply from Aunt Marjory.

Dutton did not receive an invite from me. The shifters?

Annabelle screwed up her face. *Not from Gabriel's reaction.*

Then how?

Good point. The only people who knew about the meeting were her, Aunt Marjory, Gabriel and Stefanie — Stefanie didn't appear to like Dutton any more than Annabelle — and Isobella. There was no way Isobella would have given Dutton that information. She knew how much Annabelle despised him. And Isobella wasn't fond of him, either.

I don't know, but I think we really need to find out.

Annabelle flicked through her contacts for Isobella's number. Facing Gabriel on her own was bad enough, but Dutton as well was beyond her forbearance.

Fancy a dinner at the Ritz-Carlton rather than a cheese toastie?

Isobella's reply was immediate. *???*

Gabriel's here on his own.

Oh. You think he might still have a thing for you?

Annabelle's fingers hovered over her phone. Could he? Doubtful. Though, he had been pretty into her in the High Priestess' downstairs bathroom. No. If he really did have a thing for her, surely he would have tried to find her in the last three years, or at least returned to her in Paris. She'd waited a month for him to return, and he'd never showed. Nope. Shifters were renowned for being highly sexual. He was merely taking advantage of an opportunity that had dropped in his lap, nothing more.

And Dutton turned up. Uninvited.

Groan The man needs to learn the meaning of the word no.

Don't leave me here on my own, Isobella.

Annabelle stared at herself in the mirror, at her flushed cheeks and her too-bright eyes as the silence stretched between texts.

Pleeeease.

The wait for a reply was interminable.

I'll be there as soon as I can. But you owe me. Big time.

Thank you, Isobella. You're the best sister ever.

Ha! I'm your only sister.

Annabelle slipped her phone back into her bag and straightened her dress. With her shoulders squared, she exited the ladies' room. She just had to keep from killing Dutton, or begging Gabriel for sex, until backup arrived.

Chapter Seven

Over his wineglass, Gabriel eyed Dutton. Their talk
with Marjory Jackson earlier had yielded more than
he'd expected. Marjory Jackson was looking to retire as
High Priestess. Annabelle was Marjory Jackson's niece,
and was who Marjory was pinning her hopes on as her
replacement. Dutton, the *fils de pute*, according to
Marjory, wanted the coven, not Annabelle. Gabriel
wasn't too sure about that. He'd seen the look in
Dutton's eyes at Marjory's house. The way he'd stared
at the swell of Annabelle's breasts as she'd poked him
in the chest, furious he'd dared to insinuate their
marriage was a done deal. Gabriel grimaced. Coven
politics, it seemed, were no less convoluted than pack
politics.

He glanced at his phone again. Nothing. No word
from Pierre or Louis. What he was going to do if his
Annabelle turned out to be *the* Bella Rodriguez, he
couldn't even contemplate. Stef had asked him if he
was sure she was his, and he was. Wasn't he? His leg

bounced beneath the table, and his wolf paced in his mind. He and his wolf were about going out of his skin just thinking about letting her go again.

Dutton set his whiskey on the table. "Why don't we get down to business? Annabelle cannot go on this mission. I'm sure you agree."

Gabriel hid his amusement behind his wine. He did agree, but not for the same reasons as Dutton. He tilted his head and regarded the warlock. Could Dutton be the coven's *plan de sauvegarde*? They'd suggested Marjory come up with a contingency plan, should something happen to Annabelle. Like Gabriel claiming her. Could Dutton be it? Gabriel didn't think so. Marjory had been very diplomatic, but she hadn't been able to hide her distaste for the warlock. Not completely. Not from him.

"I'll not allow it," said Dutton.

Gabriel choked on his wine. Were they thinking of the same Annabelle?

"And it's clear to everyone in the coven, with the exception of the High Priestess, that I should be the one to undertake this task."

Was it clear, or was Dutton nothing more than a *crétin arrogant*? The latter, he suspected.

Annabelle, a vision in midnight blue, exited the *toilette*. And like in Paris, when he'd first spotted her strolling along the Seine, her coffee in one hand, her camera in the other and her woolen leggings showcasing her shapely legs as she spun around taking in the view, she mesmerized him. She walked toward their table, her dress clinging to her curves as she moved. Wearing no *soutien-gorge,* her breasts bounced as she sashayed across the room.

And those boots... *Fuck me*. He wanted her naked but for them. Gabriel spread his legs a little, allowing more room for his burgeoning cock.

He followed the line of her dress, from the swell of her breast, past the curve of her hip, down to the hint of skin between the hem and the tops of her boots, giving her a thorough eye fucking. It's what he suspected she'd had in mind by wearing *that* dress, those boots and no brassiere. He was not one to disappoint. Not his Annabelle.

She slid into her seat, glaring at him, though the effect was sultrier than perhaps she intended. Anticipation sizzled up his spine. He would have his woman beneath him before the night was through.

She turned her scowl on the warlock. "Dutton, you're still here. What a pity."

Dutton clasped his hands behind his head and leaned back in his chair. "So you really think you can take on this tenth century witch hunter, Annabelle?"

It was tempting to hook his foot around the *connard's* chair, reef it out from under him and watch him fall.

Annabelle's eyes turned the icy blue of the Arctic. "Yes, Dutton, I do. Now" — she dismissed Dutton with a flick of her hand — "Gabriel, what can you tell us about this Eveque Faucher?"

Gabriel leaned his elbows on the table. "Faucher is not the only danger you'll face in the tenth century. How accurate is this spell?" He took a sip of his wine — a nice Bordeaux he'd chosen with Annabelle in mind. "You have tested it, right?"

He didn't like the idea of discussing too much in front of Dutton, but it didn't look like the *connard* had plans to leave anytime soon.

Annabelle's gaze dipped, burned a path across his shirt and caught on the vee of skin laid bare by his open collar. Her pupils dilated, leaving only a thin circle of blue visible. Her breath gave a little hitch and her heart rate increased.

He bit back a grin. "Annabelle."

Her gaze snapped back to his face. "What?"

"The spell," he reiterated. "You have tested it, right?"

"Oh." She flushed, then glared at him, sending a side glance at Dutton. "Yes. Yes, of course we've tested it."

So Annabelle didn't only dislike Dutton, she didn't trust him either. His woman had good instincts.

Dutton frowned. "You've tested the spell? Already? No one informed me of this."

Annabelle snorted. "You're not privy to a lot of things, Dutton. Of course the High Priestess and I tested it. Our whole plan rests on it working."

"And it worked?" he asked.

A wariness crossed Annabelle's face, and Gabriel's hackles rose.

She thrust out her chin. "Yes. Would I be here discussing this mission with you if it hadn't?"

Gabriel brought his wolf close to the surface and reached out with his enhanced senses. He scented no lie, but... Annabelle shifted in her seat. She wasn't telling the whole truth, either. He'd sensed the same as when she'd talked of her discovery of the spell. *Interesting.*

He leaned back in his chair and crossed his arms. "How many times have you used it?"

Annabelle shrugged. "Only a few. It requires substantial preparation, and —" Her brow furrowed ever so slightly. "We may need to practice a little."

So the spell wasn't exact. He needed to get his hands on that spell. Maybe send a copy to Alain d'Louncrais, Stef's cousin. Coming from a long line of Langeais wolves tracing back to D'Artagnon d'Louncrais and his witch mate, Alain was both werewolf and witch, unique even in their pack. He might know of a way to make it more accurate. The last thing he wanted was to send anyone back in time if they couldn't guarantee where they'd end up. Not with his and his brothers' existence depending on it.

The maître d' sidled up to their table. "My apologies, sir, but there is a lady, just arrived, insisting she is part of your table."

Gabriel angled around Annabelle for a look at the woman standing at the podium. His breath stalled. Long dark hair, dark eyes and the same skin tone as his own. If he'd had a sister, she would've looked much like this. Could this be...

Annabelle turned, smiled, and waved the woman over. "Yes, she's with us. Thank you." Annabelle beckoned her friend to take the spare chair the maître d' provided. "Gabriel, this is Isobella."

Iso*bella*?

Dutton snarled. "You shouldn't have asked her here. She's not part of this mission."

Annabelle slapped her hand hard against the table. "She has more right to be here than you have, Dutton."

Gabriel leaned forward. "How so?"

"Isobella's family."

"She's a Jackson?"

Annabelle shook her head. "Yes and no. She's a Rodriguez. Our families are joined through marriage. She's my sister. Technically, my stepsister."

Gabriel wanted to punch the air with his fist. He knew it. *Isobella* Rodriguez was *the* Bella Rodriguez, not his Annabelle.

His phone buzzed, and a name flashed across the screen.

"Excuse me for a moment." Gabriel moved away from the table, and as he passed Isobella, something about her scent gave him pause. He glanced at his phone. He needed to take this call. Gabriel headed for the lobby. Isobella would have to wait.

"Pierre, what have you found?"

"Much, brother of mine," said Pierre, his voice echoing down the line. "And there may well be a few complications."

"How so?" The right Bella Rodriguez had turned up, leaving Annabelle, *his* Annabelle, free for the claiming. Nothing Pierre could say would ruin his good mood.

"The coven is a hotbed of dissent at the moment, spearheaded primarily by the King family."

Gabriel grunted. *No surprises there.*

"I'll send you the details on the King family. They're powerful, and they've made a lot of alliances lately. Their matriarch, a witch named Cordelia King… I don't know that I'd want to cross her."

That didn't sound so good for *his* Annabelle.

"Oh, and there are *two* potential Bella Rodriguezs," interrupted Louis. "Step-sisters."

Pierre must have him on speakerphone. "Mmm-hmm. Annabelle and Isobella."

"*Oui.*" Louis huffed. "You could have led with that and saved us the trouble. I'm not sure why we bother, Pierre."

Merde. "Just give me the news, you two." Sometimes Louis was a little overdramatic.

"Fine, but you owe us. We spent all night working on this."

"No, you didn't. If you had, you would've answered my call. Let me guess, you were busy horizontally. Both of you."

Pierre chuckled. "You know us too well, brother."

"We met her at *Le Duplex*," added Louis. "She had the hottest little ass I've ever seen, and that mouth of hers…well… Let's just say she—"

"Let's *not* say anything." Pierre and Louis were his little brothers. Twins. Even as children, the two of them had shared everything, and that practice had continued into adulthood. They shared an apartment, a car and clothes. And women. Gabriel didn't know how that was going to work when one of them found their mate. Probably like his ancestors. They'd share her. He'd like to be a fly on the wall for *that* conversation. "Just give me the information I need. Please."

"Testy, testy," said Louis.

"Things not going well with Annabelle?" asked Pierre.

Gabriel growled and a couple passing him in the lobby gave him a wide berth, a look of alarm on their faces. "Stef told you, didn't she?" *Bloody Stef*. She probably found his situation amusing. "Look, just…just give me the information, Pierre."

Of the two of them, Pierre was the more serious, sensible one. He kept Louis in line, for the most part.

Louis huffed down the phone line, but it was Pierre who answered him. "I've matched our family genetics through medical records to—"

"Isobella?"

"*Oui*. Though you had to have guessed by looking at her. She's the one, Gabriel. The one who mated Edmond and Aubert."

Gabriel's relief at Pierre's confirmation was palpable.

"She's where we get our stunning good looks from," added Louis.

"But..." Even over the phone, Gabriel sensed Pierre's disquiet. "We have a problem."

Ice slivered down his spine. "What sort of problem?"

"A big one."

Merde. He paced about the lobby. As if things weren't complicated enough.

"Isobella's sick, Gabriel. That's why she has medical records in the system."

Gabriel glanced over at the table. Annabelle and Dutton were arguing. Isobella sat quietly, her hands resting in her lap. The wrongness of her scent. She was ill. Of course.

"How sick?"

"It's not good."

He raked his hand through his hair. "How long?"

Pierre sighed down the phone line. "It's hard to say. The diagnosis is only recent, and the cancer is at stage four."

"Cancer? Stage four? She doesn't look that sick?"

"Sadly, ovarian cancer is often asymptomatic."

Ovarian cancer. *Putain.* It was a miracle he and his brothers existed at all.

"Take a guess, Pierre. How long?"

"With no intervention on our part?"

"*Oui*. Without a turning."

"She could have five years, she could have one. She could have less. There's no way of knowing how fast the cancer is spreading yet. But it's already leeching into other parts of her body. That means she's going to get sicker, and it's possible her doctor will have recommended surgery and chemotherapy. Neither of which will put her in a good place physically, or mentally to travel back in time."

L'enfer. He paced the lobby. She had to go. There was no way around it. "Maybe I could turn her now?"

Louis snorted. "And they say I'm impulsive."

"That could take months, and doing so will change what will happen in the tenth century." Pierre sighed. "It's your decision, Gabriel. You're there. You can evaluate where she's at physically. But if it was me... I wouldn't be messing with anything on this end. Personally, I like existing. We both do. And we'd thank you to take that into consideration when making that decision."

Gabriel eyed Isobella. She said something that made Annabelle laugh, and Dutton scowl. He grimaced. Who knew if Isobella's illness was pivotal to his ancestors finding her? In taking up her cause? In their decision to mate her?

"You're right, I can't turn her." Pierre's and Louis' relief filtered across the airwaves. "We'll just have to work with what we've got." He glanced over at the table again. Isobella was watching him. He turned his back to her. "Can you check into something else for me? Annabelle says she took a photo of the spell they're using to go back in time. She deleted it from her phone, or so she said."

"Even if she deleted it, I should be able to find it," said Pierre. "Do you have her number?"

"No." If he did, he would have contacted her long before now. The number he had for her in Paris had stopped working about the same time she'd left the country. Probably a SIM card from a local service provider she'd used while she was in France. Not for the first time, he mentally kicked himself for not answering her numerous calls and texts while she was still in Paris. Before they'd stopped altogether.

"Doesn't matter. We'll find it. I'll call you when we have something."

"*Merci.*" Gabriel ended the call. He brought up Stef's number and sent her a text.

Any luck?

Stef's reply was swift. *Some. Marjory Jackson is out at a function, and she's given the staff the night off. I have a few hours to search through her office. With all these books, it could take that long.*

Find anything interesting so far?

Quite a bit. I've sent a bunch of images off to Alain. The arcane knowledge in this room is phenomenal.

That may be, but Annabelle had given him another idea. *I've got a better lead for you. Annabelle works at a bookshop called Rarity. It specializes in rare and antique books. Annabelle says she found a spell in the back of a book. She took a photo before they sold it. I've got Pierre and Louis working on that. Some anonymous financier upstate bought it. So she says.*

A store like that should have a record of sales.

Precisely.

I'm on it.

He paused and then punched out another text to Stef before he could change his mind.

I've found the right Bella Rodriguez. Annabelle's mine.

A few moments passed, then a reply.

I'm very happy for you, Gabe. Be careful. Until they give us all the answers, we don't know who we can trust.

Noted.

His phone dinged with an email from Pierre. He gave the files a quick scan, paying the most attention to the one on Cordelia King, Dutton's great aunt. There wasn't much to go on, but what there was didn't make for a children's bedtime story. Pierre was right. Cordelia was a concern. His Annabelle needed him now more than ever. Whether she realized it or not.

He slipped his phone into his pocket. His thoughts grim, he returned to the table and slid into his seat. He eyed Isobella. Beneath the light touch of makeup, he noted the dark smudges under her eyes. Gabriel breathed in, taking in her scent and focusing his enhanced senses on her. Undeniably present, the taint of her illness filled his nose. His gut tightened. They had to prepare her for the tenth century, for Faucher. And make sure the spell was as accurate as possible. But first, they had to convince Annabelle not to go, and to send her step-sister instead. Her *sick* step-sister. *Putain.*

Chapter Eight

Annabelle sipped her wine, her meal sitting heavy in her stomach. She'd not missed Gabriel's interest when she'd introduced Isobella. Nor his gaze returning unerringly to her sister throughout the meal. Unlike the heat in his eyes when he looked at her, there was...concern and...awe. What was up with that? Did she even want to know? Or was she seeing things that weren't there, because having Gabriel here was messing with her state of mind? She wasn't normally the jealous type.

And Dutton... Annabelle pursed her lips. How the hell had he known about this meeting? Now more than ever, she was glad she'd kept the book a secret, even from Aunt Marjory. She'd have to move it and find somewhere more secure. Maybe she could take it back to Rarity. One book among many, it would be easy to conceal.

"You'll need to practice your French," said Gabriel. "They speak an older, mostly forgotten dialect, but you'll be able to understand them well enough."

"My French is a little rusty," admitted Annabelle.

"I can help you," offered Isobella.

Annabelle's eyebrows shot up. "You speak French?"

Isobella grinned. "The French teacher at Flintridge Sacred Heart was cute. French was one of my best subjects."

Gabriel beamed at Isobella. "Excellent. That will save a lot of time."

Really? Annabelle would refresh her French no faster with Isobella than if Gabriel taught her.

"And we'll need to get some clothes made for you, clothes that will help you blend in," said Gabriel, his focus, again, not on Annabelle, but Isobella.

Her chest tightened and her stomach churned. No, she wasn't imagining things at all. With one look at Isobella, had he moved on already? If the man could walk away from her on Christmas Eve, it wasn't a stretch to imagine a pretty face could distract him.

"One of our coven is a seamstress," interjected Annabelle, trying to draw Gabriel's gaze. Isobella didn't need any more heartache. And *she* didn't need to have her ex-lover stopping by for a tryst with her sister while she slept in the next room. "She can make anything we ask her to."

Dutton smirked. Annabelle shot him a look that promised she'd disembowel him at the earliest opportunity.

"Good. That's a start then." Gabriel leaned back in his chair, his arms crossed.

Beneath the table, a foot brushed against hers. Annabelle tensed. Dutton's? Gabriel's attention swiveled to her, and a lazy, sexy grin curled at the corners of his full lips. Kissable lips. She knew what he was capable of with that mouth.

She jerked her foot away and took a gulp of wine, anything to douse the fire that was building in her body. Gabriel lifted his nose and sniffed the air. His grin bloomed into a knowing smile, and Annabelle's cheeks heated. He dipped his gaze down her body, a not-so-subtle slide from her face to her breasts. Her nipples peaked, and she squirmed in her seat.

Damn it. She *should've* worn a bra. She'd thought only to taunt Gabriel, but now, seeing his gaze fixate on her breasts…she was the one in trouble.

Annabelle glared at him. He let out a low chuckle, and that made her squirm in her seat even more.

His chest heaved, his nostrils flared and his grin slipped. He abruptly stood. "I think we've done enough tonight." He signaled the server and settled the bill.

Relieved, Annabelle slid from her seat, and they all collected their coats and scarves before heading to the lobby. She had much to think about. Gabriel had given them a lot of information about what she could expect in the tenth century. As grim as it sounded, she was still going. Annabelle couldn't let her family down.

At the elevators, Gabriel halted and pressed the button. He took Isobella's hand and something twisted in Annabelle's chest. They even looked alike. Similar coloring, that same dark curly hair. If Annabelle didn't know otherwise, it would be easy to mistake them as siblings.

"It was an honor meeting you, Isobella. I would like to spend more time getting to know you, but if that opportunity does not arise before our time is up, then *voyager en toute securitie*."

Anabelle frowned. Her French *was* a little rusty, but she thought he'd said safe travels. *What an odd thing to say.*

Gabriel squared off with the Kings' pride and joy. "Dutton."

Dutton nodded, his face pinched tighter than a cat's asshole.

The elevator doors opened, and Gabriel beckoned out the operator. "Would you be so kind as to organize a cab each for Miss Rodriguez and Mr. King, please?"

"Of course, Mr. Montagne."

Before Annabelle could wonder at her exclusion, Gabriel dipped, grasped her by her thighs, flung her over his shoulder and stepped into the elevator. The closing doors cut off Annabelle's squawk, leaving her with a brief glimpse of Isobella's surprise and Dutton's outrage. Gabriel reached out, swiped his pass key and stabbed two buttons on the panel.

The penthouse?

"Gabriel, put me down!" She dropped her coat, scarf and purse and slapped his back, hard, but he barely flinched. "Gabriel!"

"*Belle,* must you shriek so loudly?" He slid her down his body, set her on her feet and pressed her against the elevator wall. "All you have to do is ask."

She planted her hands on his chest to push him off, ignoring the urge to curl her fingers in his shirt. God, the man not only looked good in black, he felt good in black. He'd feel better in nothing. She shut her eyes against that image, but she couldn't shut out the feel of his body against hers, the hard planes of his chest and the harder press of his cock against her stomach. Her traitorous body burned for him. Lord, it was like the fourth of July in her panties.

"Gabriel." She opened her eyes and tried for calm, but her voice wobbled.

He dipped his head into the crook of her neck and ran his nose along the sensitive skin of her throat. Her knees quivered and her determination wavered. A growl rumbled in his chest, and his musky scent filled the elevator.

"Gabriel, this is… We can't… I can't…"

Why isn't my mouth or *my brain working?*

"We can, *Belle.*"

He tugged her dress up her thighs until it bunched around her hips, and he slipped his knee between her legs. One large hand brushed against the underside of her breast, eliciting a moan. Annabelle clamped her lips together. They shouldn't be doing this. He'd left her once. She couldn't survive it happening again.

"I have a mission to prepare for, then… Then you'll be gone again." Annabelle squeezed her eyes tight, mortified at the stark vulnerability in her voice he couldn't fail to hear.

He nuzzled her ear. "*Ma Belle,* I made an oath to myself the moment I saw you in your High Priestess' office."

He sucked on her ear, and the sensation zipped like a rocket to her clit. Her head thudded against the elevator wall as he nipped his way along her jawline, and it was all she could do not to rub herself against his thick thigh.

He paused, his lips hovering over hers. So close and yet so far.

"Look at me, Annabelle."

She sucked in a shaky breath. She opened her eyes, and was drowning, drawn into him by the intensity of his liquid brown eyes and the carnal delights they promised.

"I vowed that even if I had to follow you into the past, I was never leaving you again. *Tu es à moi et seulement à moi, Belle. Pour toujours.*"

Then he claimed her mouth, delving deep, and any hope she had of resisting this, resisting him, vanished with the press of his lips and the swipe of his tongue. His hand found its way to the zipper of her dress, releasing it. Her dress sagged, and he tugged at the neckline, dragging it down. And she let him. Helped him push it down, baring her breasts to his hungry eyes. She should stop this now. Pull up her dress and press the elevator button for the lobby, the ground floor, anywhere but here. She shouldn't want sex with the man who'd ghosted her three years ago, but she did. And that confused the hell out of her. Her head was saying no, her heart...maybe. Her body—hell, yes!

The elevator dinged, the doors swished open, and Annabelle threw her arms around Gabriel's neck and her legs around his body. Tomorrow. She would worry about the stupidity of this tomorrow. Tonight, she wanted him, needed him, as she'd never needed another man before him or would after him. To hell with the consequences.

Chapter Nine

The elevator doors opened on the lobby of the penthouse suite and Gabriel rushed Annabelle into the vestibule. He didn't want to give her time to think, time to change her mind. Her hot little mouth on his throat, her hands working at the buttons on his shirt and the vice-like grip of her thighs around his hips suggested he had no cause for concern. But he wasn't taking any chances. His balls had been bluer than the stripe on his country's flag all afternoon, and he didn't think his cock could take another rejection.

"My purse, my things."

Gabriel grunted, and rushed back to the elevator, using his foot to drag Annabelle's coat, scarf and purse out before the doors whooshed closed. He retraced his steps through into his suite and kicked the door shut behind them, stumbling past the furniture until he had her pressed against the glass of the floor to ceiling windows. The lights from the San Francisco skyline twinkled behind her, but he paid them no mind, hitching her higher and ducking his head, taking her nipple in his mouth.

She pushed at his shoulders. "Wait, Gabriel."

He growled his displeasure and nipped at her nipple. Her thighs clenched tighter, and she let out a lusty moan. His Belle had always been vocal in bed.

"Stop. What about Stefanie?"

He released her nipple, and her grip on his waist loosened. She slid her feet to the floor and tugged at her dress.

"What about Stef? I told you we are not together."

"But I still don't want her to walk in on us."

Gabriel brushed her hands away, bunched the material of her dress, slid her arms free and tugged it down over her hips, dropping it into a puddle of blue at her feet.

Putain, she was beautiful. Naked but for the scrap of blue lace between her thighs and her knee-high boots.

She stiffened in his arms. "Gabriel—"

He spun her around so she faced the view—the view of her almost naked perfection. "Do you see what I see, *mon amour*?"

He nibbled at her earlobe, watching in the reflection as he slid his hand around to cup her breast. The sight of her pale creaminess against the black of his jeans, his shirt, had his balls throbbing. He pressed his body against her, sucking in a breath as she ground her ass into his groin. If he were already naked, he'd be unable to hold himself back. Though the material of his pants chafed, it kept him in check. Three long years… Annabelle wasn't ready yet for the rough fucking he needed.

"*Mon amour*, Stef is out enjoying all that San Francisco has to offer. She will not return until morning."

Did he feel guilty about the lie? Hell yes, but Stef was right. Until they had all the answers, they couldn't completely trust anyone. Annabelle had lied to him twice already this evening.

He plumped her breast, and a plume of her arousal scented the air. "Any more concerns before I give you what your body is crying out for?

Her breath hitched. "What about...protection?"

"Don't need it."

"Wha—"

He pinched her nipple, rolling it between his thumb and forefinger, and her words morphed into a throaty moan.

"The wolves of Langeais are werewolves, in the true sense of the word, Annabelle." In ways she was not ready to know the full truth of. "Like all shifters, we cannot carry diseases, but unlike other shifters, we cannot procreate with humans. I don't need to wear a condom."

Putain, he had wanted to fuck her bare from the moment he'd met her. With her very human concerns about protection, and so early in their relationship, she hadn't been ready to hear what she was to him. He'd worn a prophylactic. *Every. Damn. Time.* Not tonight.

His lips brushed her ear. "Tonight, Belle, I'll be just us. My cock, your pussy and no barrier in between."

She gasped, and the scent of her arousal intensified. She made to turn around, but he held her firm. "*L'amour de ma vie*, do you see how beautiful you look in my arms?"

He dropped a kiss at the crook of her neck, his tongue flicking out to taste her. A growl rumbled up in his throat, and his wolf pushed to the surface. It had always been this way with Annabelle. Struggling to maintain his control. To keep his wolf in check.

He met her gaze in the reflection. "Watch," he whispered, and then he tweaked her nipple with his fingers.

Her back arched, pressing her breast into his palm and her ass into his cock. He rotated his hips, grinding against her, never taking his eyes off her. Allowing the wolf through, just a little, he snagged the band of her panties with a claw and cut through the lace. They fell to the floor with her dress. He willed his wolf away, before it had a chance to take hold or push through his defenses.

She trembled as he brushed his hand over her hip, across her stomach and down, his fingers questing for her clit. Her body jerked when he found it, her mouth parting and her head sagging back against his shoulder.

"*Non, non, ma belle.* Watch."

Hooded eyes met his, then her gaze dropped to the reflection of his hand sliding through her slick folds. He thrust a finger inside her, then another, his other hand plumping her breast. Her pussy fluttered around his fingers. She was as primed as he was. With a slow slide, he pulled his fingers almost all the way out. She whimpered and her bottom lip trembled. He thrust back in, going deep.

"Yes!" she hissed.

He did it again.

"More."

L'enfer, he loved how demanding she was. He slid his fingers out again. This time, she chased them. He chuckled and scraped his blunt human teeth against the tendons of her shoulder. *La mien. Mine.* His wolf pushed forward, and his gums ached with the press of his canines. His wolf wanted to claim her, mark her as his for the world to see. For that *connard*, Dutton, to see. He resisted the urge. Not yet. Not now. Soon.

"Gabe, I need…" She ground back against his groin. "More. Now."

He understood her impatience. If he didn't free his dick from the stranglehold of his pants, he might soon cut off his circulation.

"*Oui*, so do I."

He thrust his fingers back in and set up a rhythm, fast and furious, reveling in the sounds of desperate need spilling from her mouth and of his fingers pummeling her eager pussy. With a grind of his thumb against her clit, she came, spasming around his fingers. In the reflection, her body quivered, her skin flushed, and she crushed his olive-skinned hand between her white silken thighs. He growled, setting off another spasming of her pussy. Gabriel had never seen a more beautiful sight.

Annabelle slumped against Gabriel, her body spent. She would have fallen to the floor like a limp noodle had his arms not held her in place. Residual spikes of pleasure flickered through her body as her chest heaved and her heartbeat pounded loud in her chest. Her eyelids fluttered open.

The view from the penthouse was stunning, but it was their reflection that held her attention. Her naked. Gabe still dressed. His fingers still inside her. Coffee-brown eyes reflecting back at her in the glass. Heat zipped through her, and her pussy tightened on his fingers. She whimpered. Dark shadows flitted in his eyes and his face pinched tight. His wolf was hungry.

For her. Her mouth went dry and her pussy spasmed again. His fingers weren't enough. She wanted more.

He removed his hand and stepped back.

"Gabe…"

"Don't turn around. Hands on the glass, *bebe*, and spread your legs."

She tried to swallow, but her mouth was drier than desert sand. She did as she was told, her legs wobbly in her boots. Clothing rustled behind her, and she caught a glimpse of his shirt as it slipped to the floor.

"Eyes forward."

Annabelle sucked in a breath at the guttural command. Gabriel had always been a dominant lover, but there was an edge, a rawness to him now. Was it his wolf? Had it always been there, and she'd been blind to it? No. This was something new. And, oh God, she *liked* it.

The slide of a zipper, then more rustling. Slickness coated her thighs. Soft footfalls on the carpet. Heat suffused her body, and her pelvic muscles clenched. Her thighs quivered and her nipples were so hard they were almost painful. She'd never been so turned on in all her life. A gentle touch on the curve of her hip and the heat of his palm burned into her.

"Three long years I've waited for this. I've got calluses on my fucking hand from jerking off to memories of you."

Her breathing was shallow, panting almost. Annabelle longed to press back into him, to turn around, but something held her in check. Fear? Fear she'd see her own desperate need for him reflected in his eyes?

Wait. What? Does he mean what I think he means?

A muscled thigh pushed between her legs, the brush of his cock against her ass almost bringing her undone. "Wider."

Her heart did a little skip. Had he really not slept with anyone since Paris?

He growled and slapped her ass with his palm. "Wider, Annabelle."

Heat ripped through her, bringing her to the edge. It was all she could do to get her trembling legs to comply. His fingers traced the length of her spine, and she arched her back, presenting to him.

A harsh intake of breath and a low rumble reverberated behind her. "Look at you, your pussy all pretty pink, swollen and wet. Just for me."

"Gabe…" She all but moaned his name, angling her hips higher, wanting, needing him to fill her up.

He tugged at her hips, and the thick head of his cock pressed against her entrance. "Belle, you ruined me for all other women."

Then he thrust into her, seating himself deep. She cried out at the exquisite pleasure, at the fullness, at the way he stretched her. He was a big man, in all ways, and she reveled in it.

"Prepare yourself, *mon amour*. I have waited too long for this. I'm going to fuck you like I need to. Like the animal I am."

He drew back, a delicious slide against sensitized nerve endings. Then he slammed back in. Hard. Savage. Deep. Another slide out, another deep thrust and a part moan, part scream slipped from her lips. As though all restraint lifted with her cry, the beast released, Gabe pounded into her with a relentless savagery.

Oh God, oh God, oh God!

She pressed her heated face against the icy window, and her breath fogged up the glass. Sounds she never thought she'd make again filled the room, with the accompanying slap of skin on skin and Gabe's harsh breathing. Her hands against the window and his bruising grip on her hips were the only things keeping her upright.

Putain. He'd forgotten how good this felt. The slap of his heavy balls against her thighs. The slide of his cock through her wet heat. Her little gasps and whimpers. The trembling of her pussy around his shaft. There was no feeling in the world like it. Even better, there was no barrier between his bare cock and her pussy. Finally, *finally*, he was back where he belonged. He wanted to howl his triumph to the world. The barest thread of sanity was all that kept his wolf in check. Was all that stopped him from letting it loose and bringing the hotel staff, and the authorities, down on their heads.

Against his will, his canines punched through his gums. The urge to bite her, to turn her and to truly make her his, was excruciating. He slipped his hand around to pinch her clit and a hoarse scream ripped from her throat, her pussy clenching his cock like a vise. Pleasure ripped up his spine, and he thrust one last time. His body stiffened, spots danced in front of his eyes, and he threw his head back and roared his release, spilling his seed inside her.

Merde. He had died and gone to heaven.

Annabelle collapsed against him, trembling, and he folded his big body around her, taking them both to the floor. Still inside her. Still impossibly hard. Annabelle still wearing those sexy boots. He cradled her in his arms as he tried to catch his breath and slow his pounding heart. *Putain.* It had always been good between them, but that...

"Wow," she breathed, her chest heaving against his. "That was..."

He chuckled. "Mind blowing?"

"Yeah."

"*Oui*, it was."

She chuckled. "I don't think I can move."

The night was still young. Gabriel wasn't done with her yet. He didn't think he'd ever be done, but tonight... Tonight was all about making up for lost time. For those three agonizing years they'd spent apart.

He eased out of her and got to his feet. Scooping her up, he cradled her in his arms, as he padded across the room and up the floating staircase to the master suite.

There, he laid her on the bed. "Stay," he growled. "We're not finished here, Belle."

Chapter Ten

Annabelle stayed. She had no intention of moving, her body pleasantly limp and satiated. Finally. Since the moment she'd stood across from him in Aunt Marjory's study, the craving to have him had plagued her. Now it was satisfied. For the moment, at least.

Her gaze followed Gabriel's taut ass as he disappeared into the bathroom. She closed her eyes and languished on the lush comforter, her body still tingling from two mind-blowing orgasms. There would be more. Gabriel always had had the stamina of a prize bull. It made perfect sense now. Shifter genes and all that.

She frowned. In the heat of the moment, she'd trusted him when he'd said they didn't need to use a condom. They'd used them in Paris. Every single time. They'd blown through so many packets of the damn things she should have bought stocks in the company. Were they simply a part of his deception? Keeping his true nature from her?

She pushed herself up on her elbows. He'd said he couldn't procreate with humans. Was *that* why he'd left? And what had he meant by the wolves of Langeais were werewolves in the true sense of the word? In what way were they different from other shifters? Other than their supposed inability to not get humans pregnant. She needed to look into that. Maybe Aunt Marjory knew something. Or one of the shifter packs known to the coven.

"You're thinking very hard there, *ma chérie.*" Gabriel leaned against the doorway, a wet cloth in his hands.

Lord, the man was a piece of art. A Michaelangelo sculpture in the flesh. Six feet four inches of gorgeous, chiseled flesh. Her stomach fluttered. Once with Gabriel would never be enough. After tonight, would she be able to walk away?

"Just thinking about the mission," she lied.

"Mmm." He pushed off from the door frame and propped on the edge of the bed. Dipping the warm, flannel between her legs, with gentle strokes he cleaned her. "If you say so."

Annabelle flopped back on the bed, surrendering to his ministrations and his gentle steady hands. With the flannel over his thumb, he rubbed against her clit and her body came alive again, arching into his hand.

"Gabe." The word was little more than a breathless entreaty.

"I hear you, *bebe.*"

The cloth disappeared and his bare hands settled on her thighs, trailing down her legs to her boots.

"*Putain, j'adore ces bottes.* I think I'll have you wear them every time we have sex."

Laughter bubbled up in her chest. They were her favorite boots, too, and she had worn them with

Gabriel in mind. She'd wanted to tempt him, wave in front of him what he'd chosen to discard. She'd planned to show him what was no longer his, and when she had him eating out of the palm of her hand, walk away from him with a sashay of her hips and a jaunt in her step. Yeah, that had worked out well.

Gabriel moved to the end of the bed, grasped her ankles and tugged until her naked ass was on the very edge. Then he sunk to his knees, spread her thighs and draped her legs over his shoulders.

God, the sight of him between her legs, his dark eyes fixated on her core... Could she orgasm from a simple look?

"Sexy boots, pretty pussy." His hot breath puffed against her swollen lips.

She just might.

"All mine."

Then he put his mouth on her, and Annabelle knew the true meaning of the word ecstasy.

* * * *

Tucked against him, her breathing soft and steady, his mate slept, worn out by their marathon of sex. Her face, her expression soft in repose. No stubborn jutting of her chin, or flash of defiance in her eyes. He loved her sass, her independence and determination. He trailed a hand down her arm, and she stirred, murmuring in her sleep before settling again. But it was moments like these he truly treasured, where she lay soft and pliant in his arms. It was only here, in the bedroom, she let him take care of her. Where she dropped her guard, revealing a different side to the feisty Annabelle she showed the rest of the world.

He pressed a soft kiss on her head and she rolled over, her eyes fluttering open. With his large hand, he cupped her cheek, touching his lips to the top of her nose. Her gaze drifted to his leather wrist cuff, and her eyebrows dipped into a frown.

Annabelle placed her hand over his and leaned into his palm. "What if they're right, Gabriel?"

Cornflower-blue eyes met his, full of uncertainty, and he swore vengeance on the person who'd put it there. "Right about what, *mon amour*?"

She chewed her bottom lip, a sure sign she was feeling vulnerable. "That I'm not strong enough to rule the coven."

"Ah, Belle. Don't take that *connard* Dutton's words to heart. He has his own agenda, and making you doubt yourself works in his favor."

"But what if he's right? All that time in Paris, not once did I suspect you were a shifter." Her hand slipped to his leather cuff, and she ran her fingers over the silver wolf. "It's right here. On your wrist. Like a flashing neon sign, and I never guessed. What sort of witch am I if I can't tell the difference between a human and a shifter?"

"Hey." He tilted her chin to look at him. "That was three years ago. And I didn't think you were ready to know, so I hid what I was. I didn't suspect you were a witch, either, and I'm head of pack security."

"But—"

"No buts, Annabelle. You're more than capable of running that coven." With him by her side, no one would dare challenge her.

"You really think so?"

Merde. He hated the tremble in her voice, the self doubt that plagued her.

"I do." Once they were mated, once she became... His gums ached with his need to claim her. He was getting ahead of himself. "And when you're High Priestess, you can kick that *fils de pute* and his whole damn family out of your coven."

"Mm, that's a nice thought."

Her gaze dropped again to his wrist cuff. Gone was the soft expression. The in-charge, take no prisoners Annabelle was back. "Why do you all wear one of these? I'm assuming you all do. Stefanie has one, too." Her eyes narrowed. "It seems, for a pack wanting to remain hidden, this is not the way to go about it. Does it have something to do with being... What did you say... The wolves of Langeais are werewolves, in the true sense of the word?"

He'd been hoping, in the throes of passion, she'd forget he'd said that.

"What did you mean by that?"

That he couldn't tell her. Not yet. She'd need to know soon enough, but he wanted to make sure she wouldn't run first.

"These wrist cuffs are a way to protect us against one of our weaknesses." This he could tell her. "Wolfsbane has a powerful effect on us. Not a good one. So, we use silver to counteract its potency."

She eyed the small wolf, protected from his skin by the leather of the cuff. "I take it silver is another weakness, or you'd all be wearing a silver bracelet, or watch."

His Annabelle didn't miss a thing. "You would be correct. If we encounter wolfsbane, we turn the cuff over. This small amount of silver burns a little, but it nullifies any impact of wolfsbane."

"Clever."

"One of our ancestors figured it out. Back in the tenth century." Could Isobella have had a hand in that? It was possible. Maxime, his alpha, would know. He swore that *connard* kept secrets for the sake of keeping secrets.

"And these followers of this Bishop Faucher's teachings, they know about the effect wolfsbane has on you?"

"*Oui.*"

She trailed a finger down his chest. "I wonder what else they know. What are you hiding from me, Gabriel?"

Nothing he could tell her right now. He captured her hand and sucked her finger into his mouth.

Her eyes darkened, and her lips parted. "Don't try to distract me, Gabe."

He swirled his tongue around her finger and her breath hitched.

"Nice try, big guy, but I still want my answer."

If the slow softening of her body, and the hint of an arch in her back pressing her peaked nipples against his chest was anything to go by, he wasn't trying. He was succeeding. He rolled his tongue around her finger again and this time he added a hint of fang.

She closed her eyes and dropped her head back. "Okay. Distract me."

Her words were little more than a husky whisper. Gabriel grinned, released her finger and rolled her beneath him. With what he had planned, she wouldn't be thinking about anything for a while.

* * * *

The weak rays of a winter's sun streamed across the San Francisco skyline as Annabelle, collected her boots—discarded after several rounds of mind-blowing sex—and tiptoed down the stairs to grab her clothes. Gabriel slept on, sprawled across the bed on his stomach, his perfect ass an almost too tempting a reason to stay. She kept moving. She didn't want to be there when he woke. Didn't want to have to deal with the awkward conversation about what this had, or hadn't, been. This time Annabelle was determined to be the one leaving.

She paused for a moment by the window in the living area, taking in the view. Faint hand prints, *her* hand prints, marred the glass, a visible reminder of last night. Her body heated, and she clenched her thighs. Hell. Last night should have been enough to get him out her of system. Sadly, no. But her body would just have to deal with it. Guarding her heart took precedence.

She turned away from the window and slipped on her panties, pulled on her dress and zipped up her boots. With one last look at the penthouse suite—*the penthouse suite*—she stepped into the foyer, gathered up her coat, scarf and purse and pressed the button for the elevator.

In the lobby, the bellhop, doing his best to hide his grin, called her a cab. She must look like a fright. Well fucked, more likely. And she had been. Her body was pleasantly sore in ways she hadn't experienced in a long time.

She gave Aunt Marjory's address to the driver and raked her fingers through her hair in an effort to detangle it at least a little. In the end, she gave up. She was a grown woman. When it came to her sex life, she didn't have to answer to anyone. Unless it interfered with her mission, or with coven business. And it wouldn't. Aunt Marjory had no cause for concern.

What was concerning, and needed immediate attention, was Dutton. If Aunt Marjory hadn't informed him of the meeting, and Gabriel hadn't invited him, how the hell had he known to be there? And while she was talking to Aunt Marjory about Dutton, she was going to quash any idea, any plan, that included her marrying that insufferable man. Gabriel might have left her in Paris. He was most likely using her as a booty call now, despite his pretty words uttered in the heat of the moment, but Annabelle wasn't so desperate to fill the void she'd consider marrying Dutton. Or anyone from the King family, for that matter.

Only last month, Cordelia King had insinuated that there were other King males she could choose from, should Dutton not be to her taste. All of them considerably older or younger. Ugh. She loved her coven, would do almost anything for it, but she'd rather spend the rest of her days wearing out the battery in her vibrator than consider marrying anyone with a last name of King.

She glanced up at the face of The Ritz-Carlton building and craned her neck to see the top floor, her memories of last night on replay in her mind. Up there, in the penthouse suite, still sleeping — *that* man was to her taste. She'd gotten more than a taste. She'd had barely three hours of sleep.

She pushed aside the images as the cab maneuvered into traffic. The driver switched on the radio and an idiotically enthusiastic version of *Jingle Bells* played through the tinny speakers. She grimaced. Only one more week of Christmas celebrations then it would be all over for another year. With any luck, she'd be so busy prepping for her mission it would fly by.

Annabelle leaned her head back against the seat and closed her tired eyes. When Gabriel left her again, as he no doubt would, Annabelle would have one more reason to loathe Christmas.

Chapter Eleven

Dutton picked his way down the street, keeping to the shadows and avoiding the rugged-up bundles of homeless people beginning to stir. He kept his pocketknife handy and a spell on the tip of his tongue. In the Tenderloin district, at this early hour, even a powerful blood witch needed to watch his back.

He scanned the street, looking for anything out of place. One couldn't be too careful, not with shifters on the scene now. Confident no one had followed him, he crossed to the dilapidated building. It had an abandoned air about it, carefully curated, with its rusted fire escapes and cracked glass front door, the ground-floor windows all boarded up.

His great aunt's ward rippled over him as Dutton pushed through the entrance into a foyer that matched the front façade. There was no need for a lock. The ward would turn away anyone not invited. All the same, blood was required to get beyond the foyer. He took out his pocketknife, nicked his thumb and pressed it to the elevator button. The doors swished open. That someone like Cordelia King, perhaps *the* most powerful witch in San Francisco, would live in this dump would never occur to anyone, but then that was the whole point of the façade. Dutton stepped into the sleek, modern elevator and pressed the button for the third floor.

The top floor of the building was as sumptuous as any home on billionaires' row. Cordelia King loved her comforts. She also liked her privacy. No one in the coven, apart from family, knew where Cordelia lived. None of them would divulge it. Cordelia's wrath was a fearsome thing. Dutton smirked. That damn shifter was going to find out how fearsome soon enough.

Plush carpet crushed beneath his shoes as he entered the sitting room. Couched in shadows, his great aunt awaited him. She was not alone. By the window, hands in his pockets staring at the street below, stood a man. His expensive suit wouldn't have been out of place in the Financial District, but there was a roughness about him, an edginess in his stance, as though he were a split second away from a brawl. Wicked scars slashing across one cheek only added to the impression. Scars from a shifter, if Dutton wasn't mistaken.

"Update us please, Dutton." Cordelia's voice cracked across the room, sharper than a slaver's whip. She might well be in her eighties, but she was no ailing octogenarian.

Dutton eyed the stranger. If his aunt was comfortable talking about this in front of him, Dutton was not going to question it. "They're sending Annabelle back to the tenth century, like we planned. I raised enough objections for them to think I'm against it. But this damn shifter, Gabriel Montagne, is going to be a problem."

The man at the window turned. "Not for long."

The man's accent was thick, even thicker than that of the two Langeais wolves. Dutton's lip curled. *Another Frenchman.* He'd had about enough of the French.

"Dutton, this is Gerard Boucher. He's a member of the Faucherians."

Faucherians? As in Eveque Faucher? Like Annabelle, Dutton had never heard of the tenth-century bishop. Not until his great aunt had given him the name and the background. Told him to push for Faucher to be the coven's target in their forays into time travel. It hadn't been easy. The high priestess was wise to distrust anything put forward by the Kings, but Dutton had been persuasive. He curled his hands into fists. *Shame persuasion hadn't fared so well with Annabelle.*

"The *Faucherians*? What is that? Some sort of" — Dutton ran his gaze over the other man, unable to keep the derision out of his voice — "religious group?"

"Yes, Dutton, they follow the teachings of Eveque Faucher," said Cordelia. "They specialize in hunting down supernatural entities."

He swiveled his gaze to his aunt. Did Boucher know they were witches?

"They're a highly motivated organization with a lot of resources."

Ah, resources.

"We've come to an alliance," said Cordelia, the unspoken 'for now' hanging in the air. "They've been hunting the Langeais wolves for centuries. We have a way to help them. And in return, they can help us."

Did Boucher realize, as soon as Cordelia had what she wanted, she'd turn on Boucher and his organization? Probably not. If the man was too stupid to see it, Dutton wasn't going to be the one to enlighten him.

Boucher held Cordelia's stare. "If you can do what you say. Control zis women you are sending back. 'ave 'er target ze d'Louncrais, not Faucher."

The man had balls, Dutton would give him that.

Irritation flickered in Cordelia's eyes. Boucher showed no signs he'd taken the hint.

"We'll uphold our end of the bargain." Cordelia's words came with a coating of steel.

Boucher shrugged. "And I will uphold mine." He turned to Dutton. "Where iz 'e now? Montagne?"

Dutton gritted his teeth. "Fucking Annabelle. They have history. Damn wolf is acting like he has some sort of claim on her." Though his blood still boiled, he took comfort in knowing Annabelle would soon be his — willing or unwilling — heart, body and soul.

Boucher cocked an eyebrow, making the scars on his face stretch. "'E iz? Mm. Interesting, no?"

"Interesting? He's *fucking* my intended. It's pissing me off, that's what it is. It's not *fucking interesting*." Dutton paced, his earlier agitation returning. The prick of a shifter had not tried to hide his intentions. He'd slung Annabelle over his shoulder right in front of him and carried her into the elevator. The triumphant smirk on the shifter's face, the challenge in his eyes as the elevator doors had closed — it had taken everything he had not to throw himself at them. He'd wanted to pound the shifter into the expensive foyer tiles and wipe them with his blood. He'd been so close to unleashing his magic right there and then, in the lobby of the Ritz-Carlton. Only Isobella's warning glare had held him in check.

Boucher remained unmoved. "She must be somezing special, zis Annabelle, no? Zis could be useful."

"Useful? *Useful?*"

"Dutton."

The warning note in his great aunt's voice pulled him up short. He huffed and made a beeline for the side cabinet. He needed a drink, and he didn't care it was six in the morning. After the night he'd had, imagining Annabelle with another man between her thighs... Dutton poured himself a whiskey, allowing the slide of it down his throat to burn away some of his anger.

"Could it be zis woman iz Montagne's mate?"

Dutton spat out his whiskey. "*What?*"

"Could it be zis Annabelle means more to 'im zan a mere, 'ow you say, *booty call?*"

Dutton wiped the whiskey off his chin with his sleeve.

"You say 'e has a 'istory wiz her? Perhaps z'ere is somezing bringing him back to 'er, no?"

Was it possible?

"Does 'e have eyes for no ozer woman, no matter 'ow beautiful? Does 'e growl when you get too close?"

"Yes." They had connections with shifter clans here in San Francisco. Dutton had witnessed the way shifter males were with their mates. Boucher was right. Everything about Montagne's behavior suggested he believed Annabelle was his mate.

"*Oui.* I zink she iz 'iz mate. Zis is good 'zing. 'Iz focus will be on 'er, not uz. She will lead 'im around by *la bite*, no?"

La bite? Dutton didn't speak French, but he got the idea. Dutton smiled and threw back his whiskey. In taking Annabelle for himself, Dutton would be taking away the shifter's one true mate. And didn't that just make his day.

Chapter Twelve

A persistent nudging of his foot stirred Gabriel from his sleep, and he rolled over.

"From that grin on your face and the reek of this room, I'm guessing someone got lucky last night. Very lucky."

Gabriel opened one eye to Stef standing over him. He flung his arm out to draw Annabelle into his arms and encountered nothing but cold sheets. His mood soured. She'd left him? Snuck out while he slept?

"Time to get up, Napoleon. There is intrigue afoot and your Josephine is in the middle of it all. And put on some clothes. It's too early in the morning to deal with any shifter naked, but one who I think of as a brother..." Stef exited the room. "I'll make coffee," she called out as she pounded down the stairs.

Gabriel forced himself from the bed, away from the intoxicating scent of Annabelle and sex, quickly showered then dragged on a pair of jeans. Shrugging into a T-shirt, he descended the stairs. What had Stef meant about intrigue? Had she found something at Rarity last night?

In the kitchen, Stef handed him a cup of coffee and he took a few fortifying sips before setting it down. "So, give me the details. What did you find out last night?"

Stef leaned back against the counter, cradling her cup in her hands. "Marjory's study was a wealth of knowledge, but I found nothing relating to time travel, spells or otherwise. Nor did I find a hint of an amulet, but" — she shrugged — "I left not long after you texted me and I hadn't been in there long. It took a bit getting past Marjory's wards. I had to call Alain for help. There could've been something there."

"Maybe. Annabelle said she sent her the photo she says she took of the spell. Marjory Jackson's too smart to have printed it out."

He retreated to the living area and collected his phone, checking for messages as he returned to the kitchen.

"Nothing from Pierre or Louis yet. Annabelle was a little reluctant about sharing information last night. Getting a look at her phone was out of the question. I didn't even have her number to give to him. Here's hoping she didn't use a burner phone."

"Alain hasn't got back to me on the stuff I sent him either," said Stef. "He's in Mosswood, Georgia, for the election to the Council of Witches. He's running in the election."

Gabriel stared at Stef. "*Merde*. Who sanctioned that? Nobody cleared it with me."

Stef shrugged. "Our alpha, I suppose."

Gabriel leaned against the kitchen counter, shaking his head. "Really? Your brother's an idiot."

Amusement lit up Stef's eyes. "I'll tell him you said that."

Gabriel grunted. "Don't. Please. It took me days to heal after my last training session with him. I'd hate to think of the state I'd be in if I piss him off. Let's just hope your brother's faith in Alain is not misplaced. And Alain behaves himself. Unlike last time."

"Agreed."

At last year's Council Christmas function, Alain had tried to seduce a powerful witch. A married, powerful witch. The subsequent fallout when the husband had found out had almost caused an international incident. They'd been lucky the witch had accepted Alain's groveling apology, claiming he'd had too much alcohol to notice the woman's wedding band. Impossible. Werewolf blood negated the effects of alcohol, and Alain's shifter senses would've told him the woman had a mate. Alain's explanation he was cultivating an image, that the witches would soon forget he was a werewolf as well as a witch if he gave them something else to gossip about, had not gone over well with Maxime. The last thing they needed was to be at war with the witches.

"So, did you find anything at Rarity?"

Stef set her cup down. "Yes, and no."

"Mmm? That sounds a little ominous."

"There is no record of a sale to any anonymous upstate financier, or any anonymous financier anywhere. I checked through the files twice. Computer and paper. They keep meticulous records — date of sale, price, the name of the book, where the store acquired said book, and the name *and* address of the purchaser. Not a single anonymous buyer of any kind."

Gabriel had sensed Annabelle wasn't telling him the whole truth, but... Annabelle had lied to him? A growl rumbled in his chest. "What game is she playing at?"

Stef held up her hand. "What I *did* find was a record of a break in a couple of months ago. The thief stole five books. Four of them, the police recovered. In the vestibule of the St Agnes Catholic church. First editions, all of them."

"And the fifth book?"

"A book of spells, touted as being from the tenth or eleventh century. Rarity's owner had it slated for assessment for two days after the theft."

Gabriel stiffened. "A grimoire?"

"That's what the owner's copy of the police report said. Here's where it gets interesting. Rarity has pretty good security measures—an alarm, security grills on the windows, cameras inside and out. Whoever broke in avoided all of them. I had help from Louis, and even then, I found it difficult."

"A tenth century text... Why didn't he have it locked in a safe?"

Stef shrugged. "Maybe he didn't think it was genuine. There were some questions around the acquisition. The guy who brought it in said he'd found it in a pawnshop. There was a notation beside that little piece of information. *Fake*—with a question mark. I couldn't find any other indication why the grimoire's authenticity was in doubt, but when the store tried to contact the owner to notify him about the theft, the number turned out to be phony."

Gabriel knew of a lot of people who'd want to get their hands on a tenth or eleventh century grimoire, especially if it was genuine. Only one of them was an employee at Rarity. "You think Annabelle's our thief?"

"It's a distinct possibility."

Gabriel downed his coffee. The hot, bitter liquid burned away some of the distaste from his mouth. "One must wonder what other spells were in that book, and who it originally belonged to. And why it ended up at Rarity. Either way, we need to get our hands on it, genuine or not."

"We do. Someone obviously thought it was authentic, or they wouldn't have gone to the trouble of stealing it." Stef reached for his cup and rinsed both mugs in the sink before setting them to drain. "You should also know, someone followed me."

Gabriel raised his eyebrows. "Someone from the coven, do you think? Or the King family. Word has it they're making a play for control of the coven."

Stef sneered. "If Dutton is the best the Kings have got, Lord help the coven if they get what they're after."

"From what I can gather, Annabelle's the one currently in line to take over from Marjory, and the Kings don't believe she's strong enough to do it on her own. I can't say they're wrong. As soon as she takes over, the Kings are going to challenge her. From what I've read, Annabelle is no match for their matriarch, Cordelia King."

"There's an easy fix for that. Claim her. Take her as your mate, turn her and rule the coven with her. No witch would be stupid enough to take on a shifter witch, not with her mate standing behind her."

Gabriel looked away.

"You haven't told her yet, have you? That we're different."

Gabriel avoided Stef's eyes.

Stef shook her head at him. "You haven't told her she's your mate, either."

"Not in so many words." He threw up his arms. "We were kind of busy last night. I planned to have that conversation with her this morning."

Stef sighed and rolled her eyes at the ceiling. "Sometimes I wonder how you males *ever* manage to get mated at all. Too busy thinking with the wrong head, that's your problem."

"Hey." He pointed a finger at Stef. "You wait until you meet your mate. Then we'll see how well you resist the call to fuck and fuck often. Trust me, talking is the last thing on your mind when you have them in your arms."

Stef chuckled. "Believe me, I'm not in any hurry to mate. I have enough overbearing, overprotective wolf shifters hounding my every step. Between you and Maxime, I can barely breathe as it is."

"Who says your mate will be a shifter? Maybe he'll be human, like Annabelle. Then you'll get to turn him and train him. You'll get to mold him exactly the way you like him."

Gabriel chuckled at the disgust on Stef's face. No, a human male wouldn't be strong enough to handle Stef. He pitied the poor shifter male who turned out to be her mate. He'd definitely have a challenge on his hands.

"Have you updated your brother yet?"

Stef grimaced. "I'm bound to get a lecture about keeping safe. I'm enjoying my bit of freedom right now, and I'm not keen to disturb my peace."

It was hard enough being a she-wolf in an over-protective pack. Being the alpha's little sister made it that much harder. Finding Nathalie, at Christmas three years ago, the youngest d'Louncrais long thought dead, had made things a little easier on Stef, but not much. "I'll call him."

"Thanks. I owe you one."

"We should split up," he said, following Stef into the living area and snagging his coat from the back of the sofa. "I'll take Annabelle, you take Isobella. We're going to need her prepped and ready to go when I take Annabelle out of the equation. The last thing we want is for Dutton to step forward and insist on going on the mission. If Isobella is already predisposed and prepared, we can send her back before he has a chance to argue." He slipped on his coat and adjusted the collar. "Do you think it *was* Dutton or one of the Kings following you?"

Stef tilted her head to the side, considering his question. "Could have been. They weren't exactly subtle. Or maybe someone wanting us to know they were there."

"Possible. You never can tell with the DGSE."

Stef quirked an eyebrow. "You think the DGSE are involved?"

The DGSE, the Directorate-General for External Security, France's foreign intelligence agency, as a whole? Maybe not. But Gabriel firmly believed someone in their ranks was poking around in their business. And so did Maxime. As chief of security, it was his job to ensure the DGSE didn't get too close.

The Langeais wolves weren't a threat, not in the usual way, to national security, but like any paranormal entity, discovery by anyone, especially the government, was high on their list of things to avoid. Gabriel shook off the sudden chill that swept through his body. To become nothing more than a science experiment, a lab rat, because of what they were, gave every shifter nightmares. With the Langeais wolves' unique ability to turn people, there was every chance the government would want to weaponize them.

In the tenth century, Lothair, the Count of Anjou, had sought to do that very thing. Their ancestors had fought against it then, and they would do everything in their power to prevent it from happening now. Keeping the balance, ensuring Isobella went back in time, that they did nothing in the present that would affect the past, was the only way to ensure not only his continued existence, but the survival of the Langeais wolves.

"It could be the DGSE." If Maxime hadn't mentioned his concerns to Stef, Gabriel wasn't going to either. "Whoever it is, be careful, Stef. It's not like we can shift here to protect ourselves."

An impish grin curled on her lips. "A wolf running down Market Street... That'd be a sight."

Gabriel chuckled and wagged his finger at her. "Don't. If you feel the need to shift, head out to Muir Woods one night."

Stef nodded. "I might do that soon."

Being in a city too long made their wolves restless. He was a regular visitor to the Meudon Forest outside of Paris. In the two months he'd spent with Annabelle three years ago, getting away had been difficult. It was a good thing being with Annabelle, being inside Annabelle, had eased his beast. He'd spent a lot of time inside Annabelle. His cock twitched at the memory.

He planned to be doing that again and as often as he could from now on. If she thought leaving before he woke would dissuade him, she was wrong. He'd spoken in French, and she may not have understood, but Annabelle was about to find out he'd meant it when he'd told her she was his forever.

* * * *

Waiting for a cab, Gabriel called Maxime.

"Where's Stef? Why hasn't she called in?"

If Maxime could reach through the phone and grab him by the throat, Gabriel suspected he would. "Nice to talk to you, too, Maxime."

"She was supposed to check in."

Gabe moved away from the cab rank and ducked into an empty doorway. "You remember she's a she-wolf, right? That she trains with an alpha. With you. And holds her own. She's capable of taking care of herself. You've made damn sure of it."

Maxime's sigh down the line was weary. "I know, but..."

"She's fine, Maxime. She's sticking close to Isobella, making sure she's prepped and ready to leave."

"Good, good." The tension in Maxime's voice eased. "So you found the right witch?"

"Yeah."

"And you've claimed your mate?"

"Soon. Things are a little complicated here right now."

"How so?"

A cab pulled up to the curb, and Gabriel waved it off. He was not having this conversation within earshot of strangers. "Well, for starters, the coven still plans to send my mate back in time. There's an ancient grimoire on the loose. The time travel spell isn't exactly accurate. Dutton King wants my mate for himself. There's a coup brewing in the coven. The King family are up to their necks in it. And from what Louis and Pierre have found, the threat from their matriarch, a Cordelia King, is substantial."

"Cordelia, did you say?"

"*Oui.* Does that name mean something to you?"

Silence settled down the line, and the hairs on the back of Gabe's neck rose. "Maxime? Is there something you need to tell me? Something about this Cordelia?"

There was a clink of glass, then liquid pouring. Gabe checked his watch, calculating the time difference. It would be around four in the afternoon in France right now. A little early for Maxime to be hitting the cognac. Whatever his alpha knew about this Cordelia, it wasn't good.

"*Oui*, my ancestor, Gaharet, wrote about a Cordelia."

"In his journal? The one that tells us about all the women who go back in time?"

"*Oui.*"

Gabriel's gut clenched. "What does it say?"

"That she's a powerful, evil witch. A time-traveling witch. If this Cordelia King is the same Cordelia, approach her with extreme prejudice. She was an enemy of the Langeais wolves back then. She'd be an enemy of us now."

Putain. Maybe it wasn't the same Cordelia, but... "Dutton King was the witch who came up with Faucher as a target. That can't be a coincidence."

"*Putain.* Have you seen this witch, Gabe? According to the journals, she has heterochromia."

"She has two different colored eyes? Like Alain?"

"*Oui.*"

"Does that mean she has the second sight as well?" Alain had inherited the ability from his medieval ancestor. It was rare and often skipped generations. And the genetic mutation was the same one that created heterochromia.

"I would imagine so."

"I haven't seen her, but I'll ask Annabelle." Gabriel pinched the bridge of his nose. "What else have you kept secret from us? From me? Damn it, Maxime. I'm your head of security. Don't you think I should have known about this?"

Putain. If this *was* the same witch, where did that leave Annabelle? That his ancestors had not defeated her, werewolves *and* experienced chevaliers, said volumes. Annabelle couldn't hope to defeat Cordelia on her own.

"I'll have Pierre and Louis dig up all they can on this Cordelia King," said Maxime. "We'll find out if it's her. I'll have them keep you informed."

"You do that." Gabe stepped out of the doorway and flagged a cab down. "And, Maxime, don't keep secrets like this from me anymore."

He ended the call and slipped into the cab, giving the driver Annabelle's address. Nothing and no one was going to lay a finger, magical or otherwise, on his Belle. Not while Gabriel still drew breath. Annabelle needed him. More than she knew. It was time to make her his mate.

Chapter Thirteen

Annabelle stared at the mess that was Aunt Marjory's normally organized office. The Christmas tree was askew, the faux presents scattered about, and ornaments knocked from their branches and crushed into tiny pieces beneath an intruder's boot. Drawers hung open and papers littered the floor and desk. All but a few books lay strewn about, ripped from their bookshelves. Ancient and valuable tomes lay open, their spines bent backward, and their pages curled over and creased.

Annabelle's blood boiled. How could someone treat these treasures with such blatant disregard? She bent to retrieve a book, straightening out its pages and checking its spine for damage. She set it upright on the bookshelf.

"The Kings, do you think? Would they stoop so low as to do all this damage?" She picked up another book, its binding hanging on to the pages by mere threads. It almost made her want to cry. She placed it gingerly on the desk. It would need to be repaired. "Not your average burglar. Someone who knew how to break through your wards."

Aunt Marjory surveyed the mess. "Do you think the shifters would do this? Gabriel?"

Annabelle raked her fingers through her tangled hair. She'd been with Gabriel all night, but... "Stefanie didn't join us for dinner, and she wasn't in their suite last night."

"And Dutton?"

"He left the same time as Isobella."

Aunt Marjory's steely gaze locked on to hers. "I ask again, do you think the shifters could have done this?"

Annabelle picked up another book, smoothed out its pages and placed it carefully back on the shelf. She didn't want to think they'd do this, but... "They were pretty keen to know about the spell."

Annabelle froze in the act of picking up another book. *The grimoire!* Was it safe in her apartment? Was Isobella safe? She would've gone straight home last night. Annabelle dug into her bag for her phone and dialed Isobella's number.

The phone rang and rang, and Annabelle's anxiety rocketed. Finally, a sleepy voice answered. "Hello."

"Isobella, are you okay? Did the apartment get burgled last night?"

"Wha— Just a minute." Muffled sounds in the background, a yawn. "Okay, now I'm up... What are you talking about?"

"Aunt Marjory's office got burgled last night. I thought when they didn't find what they wanted..." Annabelle moved the phone from her mouth and raised her eyebrows at Aunt Marjory. "They didn't get what they wanted, did they?"

"Of course not. I deleted the copy of the photo you sent me before you'd even left my house."

Annabelle's eyes widened. "You printed it out?"

"No. Keeping something that important in my office would be foolhardy. What with the way the Kings are at the moment."

Annabelle gulped. She'd been stupid enough to store the grimoire in her dresser drawer. "But...what if I'd lost my copy?"

"Really, Annabelle. I'm disappointed you think I'm such a simpleton. That I wouldn't deduce the illuminated manuscript from the French monastery was nothing more than a story. A spell like that had to have come from a grimoire. One which I'm sure you still have in your possession." Aunt Marjory's gaze bored into her. "I think you did the right thing stealing it from Rarity. We couldn't possibly let something like that fall into the wrong hands, now, could we? Mmm?"

Hell, was she that transparent?

"Hello. Hello. Annabelle. Are you still there?"

Annabelle turned back to her phone. "Sorry, Isobella. Has the apartment been broken into?

The coffee machine clicked on, grinding away in the background. "Nope. It's all fine here."

The tension eased from Annabelle's shoulders. "Okay, good. I'll be home soon."

"Well, I've got to go to work, so I might not be here when you get back." The fridge door opened. Silence. "Oh, damn." The fridge door closed, and the coffee machine abruptly shut off. "Can you pick up some milk on your way? We're out."

"Sure." Milk was the least of her concerns. "See you tonight."

She hit end and turned to Aunt Marjory. "I have to go. I'll come back later and help you clean up."

Aunt Marjory waved her off and began sorting through the papers on her desk. "I'll get the staff to help me. You focus on the mission."

At the door to the study, Annabelle paused. "There's something about the Langeais wolves you should know. They're different from other shifters somehow. Last night, Gabriel let slip they were true werewolves, whatever that means. He also said they couldn't procreate with humans."

Aunt Marjory cocked an eyebrow. "Are you sure that's not simply because he wanted to have sex with you, and he didn't have any protection on hand?"

Annabelle flushed. "It's possible, but I don't think so."

Aunt Marjory gave her a steady stare. "Very well. I'll reach out to the local shifter pack. Maybe they'll know something."

"Thanks." She turned to go, then stopped. "And we need to talk about Dutton."

Aunt Marjory dropped a sheaf of papers in a drawer. "I'm not going to pressure you to marry that moron, Annabelle. You know that, don't you?"

A sudden weight lifted off Annabelle's shoulders.

"But finding a suitable partner will alleviate some of these issues we're facing."

Annabelle crossed her arms over her chest. "You're not married. Why do I have to be?"

"You're not me, Annabelle. Times have changed since I took over the coven. Back then, the coven wasn't so strong. We had very few experienced witches, and Cordelia, the only person capable of challenging me, had gone to ground. She didn't show up again for another five years. By then, I'd consolidated my position as High Priestess."

Annabelle blew out a breath. Aunt Marjory was right. Their coven was stronger now — mostly thanks to Aunt Marjory's leadership — and Cordelia King was a formidable opponent. The old witch had had forty or so years to build alliances. The day would come when she'd make her move to take control of the coven. Dutton marrying her was merely another way for Cordelia to get what she wanted. When that ruse failed, her attack was bound to be less subtle. Could Annabelle take on a witch like Cordelia? Even with the backing of her family, and the families that were in their corner, there was a high probability Annabelle would lose.

Aunt Marjory sat down at her desk, looking every bit the High Priestess despite the disarray. "Gabriel would make a *very* powerful ally. Both to the coven and to you."

Annabelle's fingers clenched around her phone. Despite his pretty words, the chances Gabriel planned to mate her were zilch. He'd already left her once. Why would he stay now and support her in leading the coven? The answer was, she couldn't trust he would.

"Mating Gabriel would be an improvement on marrying Dutton. Just think about it, Annabelle."

Annabelle nodded. Anything to let this conversation drop. She'd thought about it a lot in Paris. Being with Gabriel long term. Marrying him. That was before she'd known he was a shifter. Now… Some shifters had an aversion to mating humans. Was Gabriel one of them? Probably. What shifter would want a mate that couldn't give him pups?

* * * *

After a quick stop at her apartment for a shower and a change of clothes, Annabelle grabbed the grimoire and headed for Rarity. To Annabelle, Rarity was a thing of beauty. She loved its wood counter with its nicks and scratches, the creak of its polished timber floors, the ladders leaning against the shelves, and the faint musty smell of old books. In an age of Kindles and eBooks, Rarity was...well...a rarity. A bookshop, but not just any bookshop.

Floor-to-ceiling bookshelves lined the store, filled with books—large, small, hardcover and paperback. Antiquarian books, out of print books, signed copies, leather-bound books and limited editions—all of them special in some way. Glass cabinets displayed the more expensive and the more fragile ones. The one nearest to her housed an incunabulum—an early printed book from the sixteenth century—seated on a frame, its pages open. On the counter, another stand with a first edition Charles Dickens. She tolerated the discrete Christmas decorations—a single, tastefully decorated tree—because in here, it was all about the books.

She'd just finished warding the grimoire disguised as a Christmas present under the Christmas tree as the shop doorbell tinkled and Gabriel walked in. Freshly showered, the hint of his aftershave tickling her nostrils, he looked... Annabelle strode back behind the counter, putting a much-needed barrier between them. How could a man look so damn sexy in a simple white tee, black jeans and a leather jacket?

Finger-combed wet hair flopped over one dark eye as he took in the store. What would Gabriel think of it? Would he shrug it off as just another store? One filled with dusty old books that no one read anymore? She rolled her lips. Why did she care what *he* thought? She never let any of her other lovers' negative opinions bother her.

Gabriel strolled into an aisle, his hands caressing the spines of the books. He picked one out and carefully opened it, flicking a few pages before placing it back on the shelf. He moved further along. Another book caught his eye.

The book in hand, he turned to look at her. "There's some pretty special books in here, Annabelle." He popped the book back on the shelf and retraced his steps.

"I think so," she said, stepping back from the counter as he leaned against it.

"You left before I woke. No morning coffee, no goodbye kiss." There was a hint of rebuke, despite his teasing tone.

Annabelle shrugged. "Sorry. I thought that's what we did, you and I. Get what we want and leave without explanation. Did I misread the situation?"

A muscle ticked in his jaw, but he nodded. "I guess I deserved that."

Damn right he did. "Did you want something, Gabriel? A book, perhaps?"

She stared him down. She had every right to be angry. Hurt. Unless he was prepared to give her an explanation right here, right now, he could remain on the other side of that counter forever, as far as Annabelle was concerned.

His nostrils flared, and he looked like he might take up her challenge, then he turned toward the rows of books, and the old heartbreak bloomed anew.

"How would one go about finding a book if one were in the market for one?"

So this was what they were reduced to? All those weeks spent together in Paris and now they were talking in the third person? "It depends on what book one was looking for?"

Gabriel shrugged. "A grimoire."

Annabelle stiffened. Did he know? Was it possible he'd known all along where the spell had come from? He'd said their pack had once protected a witch, back in the tenth century. Was the grimoire hers? What did that say about the Langeais wolves if it was? "I imagine covens would guard their grimoires well. We do. The chances of them ending up here, or on the open market, would be slim."

He smiled, those dark eyes of his boring into her. "But one did end up here, didn't it, Annabelle?"

"No," she squeaked. She stared down at the counter, her fingers tracing a deep scratch, its origins long forgotten.

His hand nudged her chin up. "Liar."

Damn shifter senses.

"I know about the grimoire you stole from here, Annabelle."

She pulled away from him. "How could you possibly know that?" Her shoulders slumped. If he'd been guessing, taking a stab in the dark, she'd just given herself away.

"Your boss keeps really good records. It didn't take Stef long to find what we were looking for."

There was no point in hiding the— *What did he just say?* "Stef was in *here*? Last night?" Her eyes narrowed on Gabriel. "Let me guess, she also broke into Aunt Marjory's house."

His silence was all the answer she needed. Hurt blossomed in her chest. "I get it now. While we were…"

She cleared her throat, trying to dislodge the lump that had taken up residence there. "While we were otherwise occupied, Stef broke into our High Priestess' house, into her *office*. When she couldn't find what she was looking for, she came here. I'm surprised you didn't have this place ransacked, too."

Annabelle took in a few deep breaths. She didn't know whether to be angry or to cry. "Go back to France, Gabriel. We'll figure this mission out on our own." She skirted around the counter and flung open the door for him. "We don't need your kind of help."

Gabriel didn't move. "Did you say someone ransacked Marjory's office?"

"As if you didn't know."

He shook his head. "No, I didn't know. Stef wouldn't do that." He gestured to the store. "She came here, too. Does the store look trashed to you?"

Annabelle looked around. Nothing was out of place. No books thrown about, the counter untouched. He had a point. If Stef had trashed Aunt Marjory's office, why would she not have done the same here? She let the door swing closed.

Gabriel stalked toward her. "Annabelle, where's the grimoire now? Is it safe?"

She took a step back, folding her arms across her chest. "It's a lot safer now than it was this morning."

Her phone rang, an urgent trill from behind the counter, muffled in her backpack. She moved to answer it, but Gabriel blocked her. It stopped ringing.

"Belle, you need to show me the grimoire."

"No. And stop calling me that. You lost that right three years ago."

"Annabelle—"

Her phone rang again, and she dodged Gabriel. "I need to answer that. It could be important."

She grabbed her bag, digging it out. "It's the High Priestess." She hit answer. "Aunt Marjory."

"Annabelle, whatever you do, don't say another word to Dutton or any of the King family about your task," she said.

She caught the tilt of Gabriel's head. He was listening in. "Okay, sure. I wasn't planning on it, anyway. Before you say anything more, you should know Gabriel's right here."

"Good. You can trust him."

"But Stef—"

"Annabelle, while cleaning up the mess in my office, we found an electronic listening device. That must have been how Dutton knew of your meeting at The Ritz-Carlton last night."

"Who's to say the shifters didn't put it there?"

Gabriel tsk tsked. Annabelle glared at him.

"I had Roger take a look at it. He got a partial print off it. Dutton's arrest for that bar fight a few years back came in useful. Roger matched his prints."

Having a warlock who was also a cop had come in handy over the years. Thank goodness Roger was on their side of the coven divide, not the Kings'.

"But I still don't think we can completely trust—"

"I've received word back from the shifters, Annabelle. What I said earlier about Gabriel being a good ally, about being a wise choice… I stand by that. In fact, now I'm openly encouraging it."

What the hell, Aunt Marjory?

Gabriel stood in front of her and rocked on his heels, arms folded, eyes twinkling and his lips curled at the corners. What she wouldn't give right now, to wipe that smug, shit-eating grin off his face.

Chapter Fourteen

Annabelle turned away from Gabriel, more to hide her own expression rather than to stop him from listening in. His shifter senses were too good. He'd hear her even if she whispered.

"What exactly did the shifters say, Aunt Marjory?"

"Honestly?" Aunt Marjory sighed. "Not much. What they *did* say was we could trust them. That allying with them would benefit us a great deal. And if one of them were to mate one of our own, it would change the power dynamics in our coven forever. *In our favor.*"

"What the hell does that mean?"

"They wouldn't say. You'll have to ask Gabriel."

Aunt Marjory signed off after reiterating to be careful around the Kings, and Annabelle shoved her phone back in her bag. A warm body pressed against her from behind and arms reached around her.

Gabriel's mouth brushed against her ear, sending shivers down her spine. "We're meant to be together, you and me. You can't resist fate, Annabelle."

She wrested herself from his embrace. "As if you haven't spent the last three years trying."

The little bell over the door tinkled, and her boss and owner of Rarity entered the store.

He stopped in the doorway. "Annabelle? Isn't it your day off?" He adjusted his spectacles on his nose and checked his watch. "And isn't it a bit early?"

"Morning, Brian. Yes, you're right. It is my day off. I just wanted to finish that catalog I was working on." She slipped her arms into her coat, wrapped her scarf around her neck and grabbed her bag, slinging it over her shoulder. "It's all done, and now that you're here, you can help this gentleman." She gestured to Gabriel. "He's in the market for a book. He mentioned a grimoire." She slung a smirk at Gabriel. "I'll see you Monday, Brian."

With a triumphant bounce to her step, Annabelle slipped from the store and out into the street, laughing to herself at the look of consternation on Gabriel's face. She hoofed it down the sidewalk. She didn't have long. Gabriel would waste no time coming after her, and she had to get to the next block where she'd parked her car.

She made it, and still no sign of the shifter. *Good.* Unlocking her door, she swung it open, only to have it slammed shut by an olive-skinned hand.

"You can't get away from me that easily, Annabelle."

Damn it. She should've walked faster. She should've run.

"We need to talk." He took her keys, guided her around to the passenger side, and opened the door. "Get in."

She thrust her chin out, prepared to fight him on this, but one look at the set of his jaw and the determination in his eyes, she decided against it and slid into the passenger seat. He probably would have picked her up and thrown her in if she'd refused. He skirted the car, slipped into the driver's seat and keyed the engine.

"And where might Stefanie be now? Searching my apartment, perhaps?"

Gabriel buckled himself in, not looking at her. "She's with Isobella."

Alarm ratcheted up her spine. "With Isobella? Why?" She spun to face him. "What do you want with my sister?" She hadn't forgotten his fascination with Isobella at dinner last night. Nothing about his behavior since then suggested he had a thing for her, so what was it? Was it some darker purpose? Had the local shifters given Aunt Marjory that spiel under threat?

He threw the car into gear. "Put your seatbelt on, Annabelle. We'll go somewhere and talk."

"I don't think so." She glared at him across the center console. "We're not going anywhere until you level with me. Why are you really here? And what has any of this got to do with Isobella?"

"Annabelle," he ground out, irritation flashing in his eyes. "I don't want to have this conversation with you sitting in a parked car on the street. Buckle up. We'll go somewhere—your flat, my hotel suite—I don't care where, and I'll tell you everything you need to know. Everything you want to know. I promise."

"Tell me what this has to do with my sister, or I swear I'm getting out of this damn car *right now*."

She locked gazes with him, her hand fumbling with the door handle.

"You are one stubborn witch." Gabriel reached over her, grabbed the seatbelt and snapped it in place across her body. He gunned the engine and pulled out into traffic.

"Damn it, Gabriel."

He focused on the road, a muscle ticking in his jaw. "You're not going on this mission into the past, Annabelle. Isobella is."

"Excuse me?"

He glanced at her, dark eyes serious, before turning his attention back to the road and driving. "It's the way it's going to be. It's the way it *has* to be."

"Says *who?*"

His hands clenched around the steering wheel. "Me. I do."

She threw up her arms. "Who died and put *you* in charge of things? This is *our* mission." She stabbed herself in the chest with her index finger. "The High Priestess has set *me* this task, not Dutton, not anyone else, and certainly not Isobella. Oh, I see what this is about." She turned to stare out of the car window at the buildings as they drove past, but not really seeing anything. Typical bloody shifters. Dominant and bossy. He was almost as bad as Dutton. Telling her what she could and couldn't do. Believing she wasn't up to this task. This was a side to Gabriel she'd never witnessed in Paris.

God, she was so sick of people thinking she wasn't strong enough. The coven, the Kings, Aunt Marjory and now Gabriel. He obviously hadn't meant a single word he'd said to her last night.

Stupid, stupid Annabelle. She'd confided in him her secret fears, and he'd said all the right words, but now he was using it against her.

"You think you can come over here and tell me what to do? After leaving me in Paris? After three years and not a word, a text, a phone call, you think you have some say in my life?"

To hell with that.

"Stop the damn car, Gabriel." She flung off her seatbelt. "*Right now.*"

"*Putain,* Annabelle." Gabriel wrenched the wheel, cars honking behind them as he pulled the car out of traffic and against the curb.

He grabbed hold of her arm. "Are you crazy? What were you going to do? Throw yourself out of a moving car?" He punched the steering wheel. "*Merde.* I will explain everything. I promise. Just let us get somewhere priv—"

A screech of tires in the traffic drowned out his words. It didn't matter. She was getting out of the car right now. The smart thing to do would be to hear him out, but Annabelle was too keyed up to do the smart thing right now. She needed some space to think, to sort through the mess of emotions and thoughts in her head. To put things into perspective. To calm the hell down. That wasn't going to happen sitting so damn close to Gabriel.

"Yeah, maybe I am crazy." She shook off his grip, a loud roaring in her ears. "I don't—"

Behind Gabriel, coming straight for them, was an enormous grill. A truck. She screamed.

"Annabelle!" Gabriel roared.

Then it hit them with a screech of metal and breaking glass. The impact threw Annabelle against the door, the shattered windscreen raining down on her. Agony flared through her shoulder, her side, her head.

She was still screaming when her door flew open, and hands grabbed for her.

"Gabriel!"

She couldn't see him, her vision fuzzy.

"Gabriel!"

The hands holding her were dragging her from the car, carrying her and tossing her into another vehicle. She cried out, pain radiating through her shoulder. The door slammed, someone gunned the engine, the tires squealed and they were moving.

Where was Gabriel? Was he okay? Alive? Was *she* going to be okay? Those were the last thoughts she had before she succumbed to the fuzziness, and everything faded to black.

Chapter Fifteen

The first thing to hit Annabelle as she regained consciousness was the pain. Her shoulder was on fire, her head throbbed like a bitch, and a million sharp needles pressed into her body. She groaned. Anyone would think she'd been hit by a...well...a truck. Her eyelids fluttered open and she winced, something crusty crinkling on the side of her face? Blood? She tried to touch her face, but her hand wouldn't move.

She scrunched up her brow and moaned again. *Oooh, that hurts.*

She squinted at the flickering light bulb above her. A bug buzzed around the dim, yellow glow. On the edge of her awareness, the murmur of voices coming from the other side of the room. *Am I in a hospital? What's my prognosis? Gabriel?*

Oh, God. Gabriel. He'd taken the full force of the impact. He was a shifter, but... A sob caught in her throat and her eyes teared up. Could he have survived that? She closed her eyes and let the tears slide down her cheeks. She tried to move her hand to wipe them away, but again, she couldn't move her... No. That wasn't right. Annabelle flexed her fingers. She had movement. She wasn't paralyzed, but she couldn't raise her hands to her face.

A memory scratched at her foggy brain. Of being pulled from the car and put...no, *thrown* into the back of a vehicle. A *van,* not an ambulance. She tried moving her arms again. And her legs. Nope, nothing. Awareness punched her in the gut. Someone had tied her to the bed. She wasn't in a hospital. Someone had kidnapped her.

She blinked, blinked again and her vision cleared. Rough log walls, a small window blacked out and a low ceiling with copper pipes running the length. Boxes stacked up against the wall and a dripping water heater. On the far side, a set of stairs going up. Someone's basement? But whose?

"Annabee. You're awake?"

"Dutton?" Her voice was little more than a croak.

"You should have agreed to marry me, Annabee. We wouldn't be here if you had."

Annabelle growled at the smarmy face leaning over her. Gabriel would have been proud of her effort. Tears pricked her eyes again.

"Gabriel?" She had to ask.

Dutton chuckled. "Not even a shifter could have survived a collision with a Mack truck. He won't be bothering us. Shame, really. I was looking forward to seeing the look on his face when I stole his one true mate from him."

One true mate? Annabelle blinked back tears. No, Dutton was wrong. If she were Gabriel's mate, he never would have left her in Paris. Would he? Did it matter now? She swallowed around the lump in her throat. If Gabriel was gone? Could she trust *anything* Dutton said? Annabelle rolled her head to the side and closed her eyes. Dutton was right about one thing. A shifter couldn't survive the kind of injuries Gabriel would've sustained. Could they?

He'd been gone from her life for three years. A pain that had hummed in the depths of her heart no matter how deep she'd tried to push it down. But if he was really gone? Forever? She choked back a sob. Not now. She couldn't fall apart now. Not here. Not trapped like this. Not in front of Dutton. There was no way she was letting Dutton see her pain.

Dutton settled on the bed beside her. "Ah, Annabee, did you love the growly shifter? Sorry, not sorry. I did tell you it wasn't appropriate to spend time with other men. Now the broody shifter is out of the picture, there should be no more obstacles to our marriage."

Annabelle shuddered. If she ever got out of this mess, she was going to kill Dutton. "You never stood a chance, Dutton. And since you'll soon be dead, I'm absolutely certain I won't be marrying you."

Focus. She dug deep, past the pain in her shoulder and her head. Past the images of Gabriel—his sexy smile, his dark eyes, laughing with her as they walked along the Seine, the way he looked at her when he kneeled between her thighs—images that threatened to overwhelm her and shut her down. She was a Jackson. A blood witch. A *strong* blood witch. She would get out of this. Then Dutton was going to pay.

She rubbed her fingers together and winced. There. A particularly nasty cut. Probably from a piece of glass from the shattered windscreen. She picked at it. If she could get the blood flowing...

Dutton's hand pressed against hers. "Uh uh, Annabee. No blood magic. I know what you can do with it, given half the chance. But even if you should try, it won't matter. This whole room is warded. You'll never break out of here."

"You think your wards could stop me?" Could they? Her blood magic was powerful, but was it powerful enough?

"Not my wards, darling." Dutton's supercilious grin chilled her. "Guess whose basement we're in?"

Annabelle swallowed. *God, no.*

Triumph glittered in Dutton's eyes. "That's right. Great Aunt Cordelia has a vested interest in our union. So, you could try to best her wards, but all you'll probably do is waste more of that precious blood of yours."

He brushed his hand across her injured forehead. Annabelle recoiled.

"Personally, I'd rather you save it for when we join our two bloodlines together."

Annabelle bared her teeth at him. "Never going to happen, *dickhead*. You think my family won't find me here? That they aren't already searching? That this wouldn't be the first place they'd look? Have you forgotten Stefanie? And the Langeais wolves?"

"Oh, our union will happen, Annabelle. There's nothing you can do to stop it now. They'll never find this place. No one is coming to save you. And by the end of the day, it will be too late. By then, we'll be married."

Annabelle chortled, wincing at the flare of pain from her shoulder. "Really, Dutton? You think after smashing a truck into the side of my car, then kidnapping me, tying me to a bed and denying me medical treatment I so obviously need... You think I would marry you? You're delusional."

"Oh, Annabelle. So naïve. I'd hoped you'd come around to my way of thinking. Come to appreciate what I'm offering you. I wanted to give you one last chance, but I don't need you to agree. Not now. I just need your blood."

Annabelle swore her heart stopped beating.

"That's right, my darling Annabee. Once we have your blood, we can control you. And by we, I mean Great Aunt Cordelia."

No. He wouldn't? Cold blue eyes stared down at her. *Oh yes, he would.* Fuck. She had to get out of here.

"Zhat iz enough, Dutton. Zhere iz no need to tell her all ze plans."

A man Annabelle had never seen before came to stand beside the bed, his French accent far stronger than Gabriel's, as though English was a language he rarely spoke. Beady dark eyes in a scarred face stared down at her. He slipped his hands into a pair of black leather gloves and Annabelle's heart stuttered. Every murder mystery, every thriller movie she'd ever watched, flicked through her head.

"Stop wasting time. We have work to do. Get her blood."

"Of course." Dutton stepped away from the bed and returned with a large syringe and some sterile wipes. "This is going to be my best Christmas ever, thanks to you, Annabee." He broke open a wipe and swiped it in the crook of her elbow. Annabelle thrashed against the restraints. "Hold her arm still," he snarled at Scarface.

Strong arms pressed against her shoulder and pain stabbed through her body.

Annabelle screamed, and struggled harder. "No, no, no, noooo!"

"Hold still, Annabelle, and it will be all over in a flash."

"Don't do this, Dutton. Please. I'm begging you. *Please!*"

Dutton chuckled. "I love it when you beg, Annabelle." His smile disappeared. "But it's wasted on me. With one vial of your blood, I get to have you to do with as I please. Then the coven will be mine."

The leer on his face, the sick excitement in his eyes sent a soul-deep chill through her body.

He leaned forward and jabbed the needle in her arm. "Merry Christmas, sweetheart."

* * * *

Gabriel slipped his arm gingerly in the coat Stef had brought him as they exited through the hospital's main doors. It'd taken forty-eight hours for Stef to get him out of the hospital. He'd already started healing when they'd wheeled him in on the ambulance stretcher, and they couldn't afford for him to remain there any longer. Pierre and Louis were working overtime to erase any records of his hospital stay, any test results, blood samples. Marjory had called in help from the coven and the shifters. No one wanted a shifter's blood in the hands of the authorities.

Already questions were being asked. How had he even survived the impact of the truck? And with so few major injuries? No human body could take that kind of trauma and survive. He should be dead. He *would've* been, were it not for his pack's heritage. Other shifters would have fared better than a human, but would most likely have died, too. But he was a Langeais wolf. Maxime would have a conniption if his blood ended up in the hands of the authorities.

Gabriel limped to their hire car and slid into the passenger seat, grunting as a rib snapped back into place. He may be healing, but it would take him at least a week for all his injuries to mend and for the bruises to fade.

"Have the twins found anything? Anything at all that might tell us where the Kings have taken Annabelle?"

Stef turned the engine over and pulled out of the parking space, steering her way to the car park exit. "No. We've checked every one of the premises they gave us. Some of them were well hidden—corporate holdings, shadow companies and the like—but Pierre and Louis found them. You can't hide anything from them. But we still haven't found her."

Dark circles ringed Stef's eyes. She probably hadn't slept any more than he had since the accident.

Stef sighed. "Gabriel... We don't even know if it was Dutton. You mentioned the DGSE."

He stared at the traffic as they drove through downtown San Francisco. "If it was the DGSE, I wouldn't be here now. It would've been me they grabbed, and I'd be in some top-secret research facility, being poked, prodded and dissected. No. It has to be something to do with the coven. Dutton's involved in this. I'm sure of it." And maybe this Cordelia Maxime had spoken of. He'd never had the chance to ask Annabelle about her. "We find Dutton, we find who took her. We find Annabelle. *Putain*, Stef, she has to be injured. She wasn't wearing her seatbelt. The impact had to have flung her against the door."

He leaned his head back against the seat and closed his eyes. He could still hear her screaming his name. It was all he could think about, replaying it over and over again in his mind. He had to find her. Save her. Before it was too late.

"I should never have left her in Paris. I should have claimed her then." He thumped his fist against the dash. "I can't lose her, Stef. Not like this."

"We'll find her, Gabriel. We'll get your mate back. The twins will come through for us. They always do."

He couldn't wait that long. They'd taken her over two days ago. She could be dead already. They were running out of— Time. He sat upright in his seat, wincing at as pain radiated across his ribcage. That was it. Time.

"Take me to Annabelle's apartment."

"Why? How will that help us? I'm sensing you have an idea."

"We need to find that grimoire. We need that spell."

Chapter Sixteen

Gabriel stood in Annabelle's apartment staring at the Christmas tree, his chest all tight. There, amongst the red and green baubles, the bows and the tinsel, were the hand carved ornaments he'd bought for her at the Christmas markets in Paris. On Christmas Eve. The night he'd walked away from her without an explanation. She'd kept them.

He'd known Annabelle was missing her family so he'd taken her to the Christmas markets to buy decorations and treats. While she'd been preoccupied at one stall, he'd purchased a beautiful hand-blown glass star, as delicate as the snowflake it'd been modeled on. He'd planned to put it on top of the tree he bought for her once she was asleep, and surprise her in the morning. He'd never gotten back to her apartment.

Instead of spending the night together drinking good wine, eating artisan cheeses and handmade chocolates, she'd spent Christmas Eve alone. And Christmas day.

He took in the angel on the top of this tree. Had she kept the star? She must have found it in amongst their parcels. Had she brought it home with her, or left it in Paris?

"Nothing in the linen closet," said Isobella, walking back into the living area.

Stef came to stand beside him. "We've searched every inch of this apartment, Gabriel. It's not here. I could go back to Marjory's and take another look, but..." She shrugged a shoulder. "I don't think we'll find it there either."

Gabriel plucked one of the wooden ornaments from the tree and cradled it in his palm. The little reindeer looked small and fragile in his large hand.

"She wouldn't have taken it into work with her, would she?" asked Isobella.

Could she have taken it back to Rarity? It would be easy to hide there. One book among many. Nobody would expect it.

Gabriel glanced at the tree. Rarity had a little tree. A tree with fake presents beneath it. That's what she'd been doing when he'd walked in that morning—standing beside the Christmas tree. She wasn't supposed to be working. It was her day off, according to her boss. She'd said she'd come in to finish a catalog she'd been working on, but she'd been standing by the tree, fussing over one of the brightly wrapped parcels beneath it.

"I know where the grimoire is." He turned to face the woman that would be his ancestor. "Isobella, do you know the preparations needed for this spell?"

Isabella nodded. "I helped Annabelle with it when she was testing it. We'll need to go out to Muir Woods. The connection with nature seems to help."

A plan formed in Gabriel's mind. "Stef, get in touch with Alain. We may need backup. Then take Isabella up to Muir Woods. I'll go to Rarity and pick up the grimoire, then I'll meet you there."

"What about the time paradox? You know, the risk of meeting yourself in the past and...not existing." Isabella chewed on her lower lip. "It's something Annabelle worried about. That and the fact she could never quite get the timing right."

Gabriel stared at the wooden reindeer still in his hand. "That's a risk I'm willing to take."

* * * *

Gabriel was grateful that Brian, the owner of Rarity, was busy with a customer when he entered the store. He made straight for the little Christmas tree by the window, with its silver and gold baubles and gold star on the top. Beneath it, artfully arranged, were a half a dozen Christmas presents, all with the same gold wrapping paper and silver ribbon. He glanced at Brian, who was talking animatedly to the customer, a book open on the counter between them. Which 'present' held the grimoire?

He sniffed, inhaling the scent of pine, old books, Brian, the citrusy musk of the customer's Dior Sauvage aftershave and Annabelle. No help there. He'd have to pick up and smell each individual book. Brian would notice that, and it may not be of any help. There was a possibility Annabelle had wrapped them all.

Brian glanced at him over his spectacles. "Oh, hello again. I'll be right with you."

Gabriel waved him off. "Take your time."

Time. He felt it slipping through his fingers. Who knew what state his Annabelle was in. Brian turned back to Mr. Dior and Gabriel brought his wolf close to the surface, opened his senses and focused on the gift-wrapped boxes. There. The one at the bottom of the pile. A subtle vibration, repelling him. A witch's ward.

He pulled out his phone and put a call through to Alain.

"This had better be important," Alain fierce-whispered. "I'm right in the middle of the election debate."

Gabriel turned his back to Brian and kept his voice low. "How do I break a witch's ward?"

"Hold on a minute." A muffled apology, a few startled exclamations, a 'this is a life-or-death situation' muttered by Alain, then Alain was back on the line, no longer whispering. "That depends on who created the ward and what its intended purpose is."

"Annabelle created it. She's a blood witch. She's placed it on a grimoire she's been hiding."

"Was she hiding the grimoire from you?"

"Yes, but also others."

"Mmm. Blood witch wards are strong. This could take time. How long have you got?"

Gabriel rubbed his hand across his face. "I don't have time, Alain. I need it. Now. Annabelle's in trouble. I have to save my mate, and it's the only way I can see to do it."

"Annabelle's your mate? That helps. A lot. Have you claimed her yet?"

"No." *L'enfer*, he wished he had. He wished he'd claimed her Christmas 2020, back in Paris. They wouldn't be where they were now if he had.

"Right. We can still make it work, but it could be a little showy, and it may hurt a bit."

Pain he could live with. For Annabelle. Showy… He glanced over his shoulder. Brian was leading Mr. Dior into one of the aisles.

"We have to be quick. I'm in a bookstore. I may only have a few minutes."

"*Putain*, Gabriel! Breaking wards takes time, sometimes days. I'm a witch, not a miracle worker."

"Maybe, but you're all I've got, Alain. I need to break the ward now. It *is* a matter of life and death. Annabelle's."

"*Merde*. Right." The thump of boots pacing back and forth echoed down the phone line. "Right. I may have something that will work. I can't guarantee it, but it's worth a try. Do you have something of Annabelle's?"

Merde. Something of… Wait.

He shoved his hand in his jacket pocket and pulled out the little wooden reindeer. "I have a Christmas ornament I bought for her."

"You gave it to her? Even better. Now, you'll need your blood."

Gabriel grunted. He set the little reindeer down next to the Christmas tree, checked Brian and his customer were otherwise occupied, then brought his wolf to the surface. His canines punched through his gums. He didn't know how much blood he'd need, but he'd bleed himself dry if it helped him save Annabelle. He punched his canines through his wrist and blood flowed from the wound, trickling down his hand and spattering on the timber floor.

"Now what?"

"Smear the blood all over the ornament."

Gabriel did as he was told. "*Oui.*"

"Touch the ornament to the object that's warded."

"That's it?"

"No. Of course that's not it. *Merde*, Gabriel. Magic, real magic, is never simple." Alain sighed. More pacing. "*L'enfer*, I don't even know if this is going to work," he muttered.

"It's all I've got, Alain. It has to work."

"Right. Let's do this. Do you love Annabelle?"

Gabriel growled, and both Brian and Mr. Dior looked his way.

He turned his back to them. "Of course I do. She's my mate. What sort of question is that?"

"And you want to save Annabelle?"

"*Oui.* Of *course.*" What the hell was up with all the stupid questions? *Merde*, he didn't have *time* for this. "Yes. I want to save Annabelle. Get to the point, Alain."

"Magic is all about intent, Gabriel. Good, bad or indifferent, your intent is important. It's what I'm counting on to make this work."

"Fine. I love Annabelle. I want to save her. Now tell me what the hell I have to do."

He checked on Brian and the customer again. They were talking animatedly about a book.

"You have to touch the ornament to the ward, but— and this is *really* important, Gabriel—when you touch the ornament to the ward, you need to keep those things, those feelings firmly in your heart and mind. It's all about the intent. The ward is designed to protect the grimoire, to keep it from falling into the hands of someone who wishes to take it from her. Someone with ill intent in their hearts. Ill intent toward *her*. Keep your thoughts focused on saving her, on your love for her."

Gabriel glanced at the bloodstained ornament in his hand, then at the Christmas-wrapped grimoire. "And that will work? Will it break the ward?"

Alain was silent for a long moment. Finally he said, "I hope so. Given the time frame. It's all you've got."

"Thanks, Alain."

"Let me know how it goes."

Gabriel ended the call and pocketed his phone. He checked the store once more. Brian was still deep in conversation with his customer. He closed his eyes and focused on his feelings for Annabelle, his mate. The way his heart jumped every time she smiled at him. How the flash of challenge in her blue eyes and the defiant tilt of her chin never failed to intrigue his wolf. How the thought of losing her made his heart heavier than a ten-ton boulder and his wolf want to howl.

He took the blood-smeared reindeer, pushed through the resistance pulsing outward, and pressed it against the wrapped grimoire. Sparks flew and fire wrapped around his arm. He gritted his teeth and locked his knees, holding the ornament in place with the sheer force of his will. A screech to rival the meanest banshee ripped through his skull, but still he held on. For his mate. For Annabelle.

All of a sudden it all stopped—the pain, the noise, the sparks—like a vacuum had sucked it all in. An uncanny silence filled the store. The noise of the traffic, of Brian and Mr. Dior, the buzzing of the overhead light—all gone. Something crackled, like a spark of electricity arcing. Then a blast of power so strong sent him flying across the room and slamming into the counter.

Gabriel slumped to the floor, his jaw clenched against the agony in his ribs. The eerie vacuum was gone, and panicked footsteps were heading his way from the back of the store. Gabriel hoisted himself to his feet and grabbed for the grimoire. He met no resistance. He snatched up the bloodied reindeer, surprised it was still intact, and raced through the door, the little bell tinkling in his wake.

Chapter Seventeen

According to the car's navigation system, Muir Woods was a forty-five-minute drive, traffic conditions permitting. Gabriel made it there in under half an hour and jagged a parking spot on his first circle of the lot. He was out of the car, striding toward Stef and Isobella before the engine had stopped ticking over.

Stef eyed the Christmas present in his hand. "You found it?"

He tore the wrapping off and held up the grimoire. "Yeah. I got it."

Scrunching up the gold wrapping and silver bow, he shoved them into his pocket as they entered Muir Woods.

Once out of sight of other hikers, tourists and day-trippers, Isobella led them off the path and they pushed deeper into the woods.

At a large tree, she stopped, dropping her backpack. "This is where Annabelle performed the spell."

Gabriel studied the forest, opening up his wolf senses. Nothing but the scent of damp earth, the rustle of the breeze in the trees and the hint of bird song. He nodded. They were far enough away from the trails. No one should interrupt them. He looked down at the book in his hand. Old and fragile, the worn binding had splotches of blood all over it, faded over the centuries to a dark brownish-red. A blood witch, like Annabelle, had owned this grimoire. Given it contained a spell to travel through time, it had probably belonged to Cordelia, the witch Maxime's ancestor had written about.

Stef and Isobella leaned over his shoulder as he gingerly turned the pages. Pages and pages of spells.

Stef grabbed the edge of the book. "It's in English. *Modern* English."

"*Oui.* And look at the spelling." Gabriel pointed to a word, then another. "*American* English. No wonder Annabelle's boss thought it was a fake."

He kept flicking through the pages.

Isobella gasped.

Gabriel paused. "Is this the spell?"

Isobella shook her head. "No. It's just... Some of these spells..." She flicked a page back and pointed at the scrawl on the page. "This one is a spell to set a person's blood on fire. It would boil you alive from the inside out." She turned another few pages back. "This one is to spread a blood-born disease. You could kill a lot of people with it in one go."

"Isobella, have you ever met Cordelia King?" he asked.

Isobella grimaced. "Once. That is one creepy old lady."

"Did you get a close look at her eyes?"

Stef raised an eyebrow at him. "What's this all about?"

"When I spoke to your brother, before the crash, he mentioned an evil time-traveling witch our ancestors had come up against. Her name was Cordelia. Apparently, she had two different colored eyes."

Isobella sucked in a breath. "Cordelia King has two different colored eyes. One blue, one green." Isobella recoiled. "Are you saying *this* grimoire belongs to Cordelia King?"

Gabriel shrugged. "It has a spell for time travel in it. It belonged to a blood witch. An *American* blood witch."

"But that would mean, all this time, our coven has harbored—"

The horror in her eyes mirrored his own feelings, but Gabriel didn't have time to dwell on it. He handed the book to Isobella. "I need the spell Annabelle used."

Isobella cringed, as if the very essence of the witch who'd once owned the book would seep through the pages and into her skin, but she took it and flipped through the pages. She stopped at the back of the book.

"There." She turned the grimoire around for him to see. "That's the spell she used." She pointed to the bottom of the page. "And that's the one she used to get back."

"Will I really need that? I'm only going back a few days."

"Then what? Then there's two of you running around for a few days?" Stef grimaced. "I don't think that's a good idea, Gabriel."

Good point. Gabriel pulled out his phone and took a photo.

"Now what do I do? Do I just make myself bleed and recite the spell?"

Stef cuffed him about the head. "*Imbecile.*"

He held out his hands. "What?"

"Alain would roll his eyeballs at you right now. Have you learned nothing from watching him over the years?"

Alain was adept at casting spells. Small, simple ones to prank his fellow wolves. Larger, more complicated ones to help the pack. Many times, Gabriel had guarded his back as he'd prepared… *Oh.*

He raked a hand through his hair. "This could take days."

"Annabelle spent a few hours preparing for it," said Isobella, "but you're a shifter. You're stronger and you heal faster. Perhaps you don't need as much prep time."

"I'll take that risk." His body was still healing from being hit by a truck, but he wasn't going to waste another minute. The most important person in the world to him, his mate, he'd failed to protect. Someone, most likely that *connard*, Dutton, had taken her from right under his nose. What was he doing with her? What was Cordelia doing with her? If Dutton was involved, then so was Cordelia King. He'd not missed the tension in Maxime's voice when he'd spoken of her. Cordelia was no ordinary witch. *Approach with extreme prejudice.*

Gabriel would do whatever it took to get her back. Alive and whole. Then he was never letting her out of his sight again. "Let's do this."

Isobella shrugged her shoulders. "Okay." She began pulling things out of her backpack—a bowl, some candles, a jar of something crushed into tiny pieces, some herbs and a few red berries in a Ziploc bag. "Candles to light your way. The bowl to hold your blood and mix the spell. Crushed snail shells to ward against witches. Hawthorn to ward against the cunning, blackthorn against the forceful and rowan berries to ward against magicians," she explained. "I've tried to cover everything." She pulled a small vial of blood from her pocket. "You'll need this, too."

Gabriel quirked an eyebrow.

"It's my blood. You'll need the power of a witch's blood for the spell to work."

"So I use yours instead of mine?"

Isobella shook her head. "You're the one going back in time, so it's going to need your blood, too."

"What about when I want to come back?"

Isobella handed him a second Ziploc bag with similar ingredients. "All sorted. You'll need to find something to put them in, but you're only going back a couple of days. It shouldn't be a problem."

With a stick, Isobella drew a pentacle in the dirt, lit the candles and placed one at each of the points. In the center, she placed the bowl and a mixture of all the ingredients.

She motioned for him to kneel before the pentacle. "Now it's your turn. You need only enough blood to sprinkle over the ingredients."

Gabriel took a deep breath and exhaled on a long sigh. If this didn't work... It had to work.

Alain's words from earlier came back to him.

It's all about intent.

Keeping Annabelle firmly in his thoughts — the winter sun on her hair, the way she tucked herself into his body at night, the fire that danced in her blue eyes when he challenged her. Wrapping himself in his deep need to protect his mate and his determination to save her, he willed his canines to drop and he bit into his wrist. For the second time in as many hours, he bled for Annabelle, letting his blood drip into the bowl and splatter over the herbs, the berries and the snail shells.

Stef gripped his shoulder. "Go save your mate, Gabriel."

Isobella stepped forward, holding the book so he could see. "Are you ready?"

Gabriel read over the spell. Seven lines. The words blood and time and body jumped out at him. "It's a little dark." Tear what asunder, exactly? Time? Him?

"Yeah, it is. The witch who wrote this book was never in line for a humanitarian of the year award. Can't say I'm shocked it was Cordelia King."

The chill of the forest settled over his shoulders, and an oily sensation curdled in his stomach. He didn't like the thought Annabelle had already used this spell a number of times. Nor that Isobella would need to use it soon. He gritted his teeth and read over the words once more. He was doing this. For Annabelle.

Isobella's gentle, dark gaze settled on him. "When you're ready, as you say the words, you need to think about where you want to be. Try to picture it in your mind. Whatever you do, don't get sidetracked."

Gabriel pictured Annabelle parking her car a block down from Rarity, and held on tight to the image, playing it over and over in his mind.

"You'll need to say the words out loud. And you need to get them right. No mistakes."

Merde. Gabriel had never been so glad Alain had insisted he be the one to guard him every time he cast a large or risky spell, watching on as Alain had prepared himself, settling himself into a meditative state. He'd often encouraged Gabriel to prepare with him. Had told him it would hone his skills, help him establish calm in *any* situation.

Had Alain known he would need this skill? That it would come to this? It made Gabriel feel a little better, a little more confident he was taking the right course of action if Alain had foreseen this moment.

Centering himself, calming his wolf, he focused on the image of Annabelle and the timing of his jaunt back into the past.

"Blood and bone and hair and skin,
Rend a hole in time so thin.
Thy body held not in place
Instead to thine imagined space."

As the words rolled off his tongue, tendrils of smoke curled up from the contents of the bowl. Berries wilted, and the herbs curled and blackened, releasing a pungent smell.

He kept reciting.

"Bleed mind and soul to point, to plunder,
To change, to bend, to tear asunder.
So mote it be."

The smoke grew thicker and the scent stronger, taking on a smell like burning motor oil. Before he could stop it, the image in his mind changed. Instead of seeing Annabelle getting out of her car, about to go into Rarity, he saw her body thrown against the door, the windscreen shattering and steam rising from the crumpled engine.

No! Putain.

He tried to get the original image back in place, but it was too late. The forest, Isobella and Stef, had disappeared and a blackness so thick it had substance pulled at him, sucking him into its depths. Pain lanced into him like a thousand knives. He gritted his teeth and let it pull him in. His body protested, a sense of being folded and forced through a sliver of time, and then being forcefully hurled forward until he slammed into something solid. The darkness leeched away, and he was lying on the pavement, his chest heaving and his whole body a throbbing ball of pain.

He groaned. *L'enfer.* Was that what Annabelle had experienced every time she'd used this spell? How had her fragile human body managed it? How would Isobella cope? He wanted to curl up in a fetal position until the pain subsided, but that would take precious minutes he couldn't afford to waste. Gabriel forced himself to his feet and leaned against the wall of a building. Where was he? Had anybody witnessed his sudden appearance?

He took in his surroundings. He was in a side alley between two buildings. Car horns blared, and a siren wailed in the distance. He stepped out onto the street, the sun high in the sky. Traffic had stopped and silence hung heavy in the air. Two buildings down, a crumpled wreck crushed by the grill of a truck, blocked the road.

He took off running toward it, mindless of the weakness of his limbs.

No, no, no, no. He was too late.

A white van pulled up to the wreck, doors flew open and Dutton and another man, a man whose scarred face was all too familiar, jumped out, reached into the wreck and dragged out a screaming Annabelle. He called on his wolf for a burst of speed, but they had her in the van before he could reach them, peeling away from him with a screech of tires.

No. He had *not* come this far to fail now. He searched his surroundings. Several motorists had stopped to help. One had left his door open, his car running, and

Gabriel didn't hesitate. He slid into the driver's seat, slammed the door and took off after the van, ignoring the owner of the vehicle running after him and waving his fist as he weaved his way through the traffic.

Keeping a close eye on the white van, he followed it as it left the city.

He dug out his phone and dialed a number.

"Stef, it's me. Listen, I don't have time to explain. Get Pierre and Louis to track my phone. I think I'm going to need backup. Dutton has Annabelle. He's not working alone. And it's not the DGSE. It's the *fucking* Faucherians."

Chapter Eighteen

Annabelle lay limp. Dutton and Scarface had gone. For now. But they'd be back, and they'd have Cordelia King in tow. No way in hell did she plan to wait around for that. Not with what Dutton had in mind for her. Being a mere puppet for Cordelia... Annabelle shivered. She'd rather be dead. With Gabriel gone...

She clenched her eyes shut tight, but a stray tear still trickled down her face. This was not the time to give in to her grief. Nor did she have any intention of giving up just yet. She was a Jackson. Jacksons were made of sterner stuff than that.

Annabelle blinked away the tears. First, she had to get her hands free. She may not yet be able to break Cordelia's wards, but she could free herself. All she needed was blood and a spell. Dutton was a fool if he thought she'd roll over like a good little lap dog.

She picked at a scab on her hand and rubbed her fingers together as blood wept from her cut.

"Release me from these binds that hold,

So my actions may be free and bold.
So mote it be."

Simple, but effective. The bindings around her wrists and ankles slid away. She leaped to her feet and crumpled to the floor. God. Getting hit by a Mack truck was no fun at all. Cradling her right shoulder, she got her knees under her and, through sheer force of will, forced herself to her feet. Unsteady but vertical, she surveyed the basement.

Yeah, the place was warded to the eyeballs. Every time she stepped near the small window high on the wall, or the stairs, the hair on the back of her neck prickled and the wards forced her back. Dutton hadn't lied to her. The wards were strong and were most likely the work of Cordelia.

Annabelle paced about the basement. There had to be a way to break Cordelia's wards. She thought through the spells she knew, discarded them all and eventually settled on coming up with a new one. Squeezing the cut on the finger, she let the blood well up.

"In this place of wood and stone,
Owned by an evil old crone,
Break down her wards into the air
And release the witch, young and fair.
So mote it be."

Energy throbbed around her, pulsing towards the window. It hit the ward, quivering against it, then flew back at her, repulsed, hitting her square in the chest and knocking her on her ass. Pain flared through her shoulder.

Bitch.

She cradled her arm, breathing through the pain until it settled a little. She groaned as she scrambled to her feet again and glared at the window.

So, that one hadn't worked. She'd try something different. And brace herself this time. No more falling over. She didn't think her body, especially her shoulder, could take much more punishment.

Four more spells, each more complex than the last, and all she had to show for it were bloody fingers and a headache to rival the throb in her shoulder. Each time she tried a spell and it failed, it rebounded on her. Either her spells weren't strong enough, or she wasn't. Cordelia was one powerful witch.

She surveyed the basement. How much time did she have left? Cordelia had to know Annabelle was testing her wards. With any luck, she'd be so confident Annabelle wouldn't break through them, she wouldn't rush over. But Dutton had her blood. He wouldn't waste time calling in his great aunt to enact his despicable plan. The clock was ticking. Annabelle had to find a way out. And soon.

Attacking it head on wasn't the answer. She needed to find a weak spot. Cordelia would have multiple layers to her wards, overlapping each other and covering any potential weaknesses. It's what Annabelle would do, and Cordelia was a canny old crone. She'd leave nothing to chance. She'd most likely woven protective counter measures into it, too. If Annabelle triggered any of them, the consequences could be far-reaching.

It all depended on how much time Cordelia had had to lay down the wards. If Dutton had been planning her kidnapping for months, Cordelia would have been renewing her wards daily, building up their strength and adding extra protections.

If, like Annabelle when she'd hidden the grimoire at Rarity, time had not been on Cordelia's side, and

Cordelia had had to come up with something in a hurry, the wards would be weaker and there'd likely be limitations to what they protected. The aim of the wards would be to keep Annabelle from escaping. If she'd been in a hurry, Cordelia would have focused on the window and the stairs. Was there another way out of the basement? An external entrance, maybe?

Annabelle turned her back on the bed they'd tied her to and the window above it. She ignored the stairs, too. That left her two walls. She used her good arm to shift a rusted old bicycle and nudged boxes along one wall out of the way with her hip. Nothing but solid brick.

She eyed the fourth wall and her last option. A set of shelves stacked haphazardly with paint tins sagged against the brick. Beside it, an old cupboard, its door hanging open on one hinge.

Annabelle started on the shelves, shifting paint tins out of the way. Behind them, all she found was more solid brick wall. She eyed the cupboard. She suspected a good gust of wind could knock the thing over. Annabelle squeezed herself between it and the shelf, put her good shoulder against it and pushed. The cupboard shifted a few inches. She pushed again, and it scraped along the floor, moving almost a full foot.

She paused, eyeing the stairs. How soundproof was this basement? Would Dutton or Scarface have heard that? If they had, they'd come pounding down the stairs any minute now. Annabelle stilled, listening, her body tense, but the door at the top of the stairs remained shut. She glanced at the wall behind her and a thin tendril of hope fluttered in her chest.

The bricks here were different. Shaped and curved, almost like... Almost like the bricks around the arch of a fireplace. Beneath the curved bricks were timber boards. Annabelle put her shoulder back against the cupboard and pushed again, and kept pushing, inch by painstaking inch, until she'd moved the cupboard a good meter and a half. With no sign of movement from above, she stood back and stared at her handiwork.

Annabelle grinned. It *was* a fireplace. At some point, someone had boarded it up, but several of the boards had rotted away. If she could get them off, maybe she could climb up the chimney. She gingerly picked at the rotten wood until she'd made a big enough gap to look through. Her smile widened. The fireplace was crumbling, and there was a small hole in the back of it, at the top just above ground level. Through it, she glimpsed the gentle swaying of the treetops.

Better yet, Annabelle didn't sense any magic. Cordelia's wards were strong. She'd expected Annabelle to use her magic to try to break the wards to escape. It had never occurred to her Annabelle might simply use her brain.

* * * *

On all four paws, Gabriel surveyed the run-down building nestled in the forest outside Fairfax. Roof shingles hung askew, some looking as though a slight breeze was all it would take to dislodge them. A tattered curtain poked out through a hole in a broken window. The porch railing bowed at one end, and half of the first step leading to the front door had rotted away. Two brick chimneys bookended the building — one covered in moss and vines but intact, the other crumbling. And parked in front of the cabin was the white van he'd followed from the accident scene.

Gabriel skirted the cabin, keeping within the camouflage of the trees. Only one door, but four…no…five windows. The cabin had a basement. That would be where Dutton had Annabelle. He edged closer to the grimy window and the hackles on the back of his neck prickled. A ward. He took cautious steps forward. The sensation of being repulsed grew. This ward was stronger than the one Annabelle had placed on the grimoire. Would Annabelle be able to break it? Would she be in any condition to try?

He opened all of his senses, searching for a trace of Annabelle. Nothing. As though the ward not only physically kept a person in, but also all sound and all scent of them, too. Or did it? His eyes narrowed on a row of freshly planted flowers along the back wall of the cabin. He snarled. Wolfsbane. Of course the *fucking* Faucherians were using wolfsbane.

If he somehow managed to get past the ward, the wolfsbane was meant to be his undoing. Looked like the Faucherians hadn't figured out the importance of their wrist cuffs. One point for team Langeais wolves. But it did confirm one thing. Something important was in that basement. Something they didn't want him to get to. He'd bet his life on it, it was Annabelle.

Gabriel slunk back to the front of the building. He sniffed around the vehicle, careful to stay in the shadows and out of view from the windows. The scar-faced man, a man he knew as Gerard Boucher, was no fool. He picked up the scents of four men and Annabelle. Dutton, Boucher, and two others — friends of Dutton's or Boucher's, he couldn't tell.

He couldn't believe the Faucherians were here. With Dutton. They followed the writings of Eveque Faucher and hunted all things supernatural, witches included.

It made no sense they'd be working with the Kings. This was all aimed at the Langeais wolves. It had to be. That two of their enemies — the Faucherians and a time-traveling witch — had created an alliance did not bode well.

Faucherians — what a stupid fucking name. Despite that, experience had taught Gabriel those who subscribed to Faucher's zealot ideals, men like Boucher, weren't stupid, and they were well trained. It was the only thing that had kept Boucher alive, though he bore the scars of their last encounter. This time, Gabriel wouldn't settle for wounding him. Boucher was involved in Annabelle's kidnapping. Gabriel was going to end him.

Nose to the ground, he circled the building again, venturing as close as he could using the van to shield him from sight of the windows. *There. Another scent.* Days old, but no less potent, the musty scent of age mingled with that of a female. He sniffed at the trace again. Beneath her scent, the taint of decay and... Could evil have a smell? If it did, Gabriel suspected this was it. There was a malignancy to it, the smell of cancerous rot, not of the body, but of the soul. Jealousy, cunning, rage and deceit all rolled into one. This must be Cordelia King. The wards were of her making.

His heartbeat set up a staccato rhythm in his chest. In all his years as the front line of security for the Langeais wolves, he had never felt the like of it. He was afraid. Not for himself, but for Annabelle. For his mate. He wanted to leap up the steps, take on the men inside and tear out their throats. Go in and scoop up his Annabelle before any more harm could come to her. *Now.*

He dug his claws into the earth and forced himself to retreat into the shadows of the forest. Nothing would be served by rushing in. He couldn't risk trying to take down four men at once. Not when at least one of them was a highly trained killer, and another capable of magic. Stef was coming, and she wouldn't be alone. He needed the expertise of the coven to break down the wards. It couldn't be too long now before she found the abandoned vehicle with his phone and his clothes inside. She would know what it meant. She would track him here.

Hang on, Belle. I'm coming.

Chapter Nineteen

Another brick dropped with a soft thud to the earth outside, and a whisper of breeze floated the scent of the forest through the hole she'd made. Annabelle paused, listening for any sound, any movement—a door opening, a footstep on the stairs. Nothing. Good. The hole looked big enough to squeeze through.

Dutton had her blood. The thought kept reverberating in her brain. Once Cordelia arrived, Annabelle's time would be up. Cordelia would perform the spell, and Annabelle would become nothing more than a puppet, a human shell with no one home inside. They could make her do whatever they wanted, tell them whatever they wanted. Then they'd have her and the grimoire.

Not. Going. To. Happen.

Annabelle, gritting her teeth against the pain in her right shoulder, pushed up on her toes and pulled her body up to the hole in the brick chimney, forcing her head and torso through. Cordelia, Dutton and

Scarface — they were going to pay for what they'd done to Gabriel. She wasn't the only person for whom Christmas would forever be painful. She'd make sure of it.

Her hips scraped against the brittle edges of the bricks, but she didn't stop, and with a few mental curses and some determined wriggling, she pushed through and fell to the ground. She grunted, muzzling her cry as her throbbing shoulder hit the dirt.

Fuck.

She lay there for a few moments, blinking back tears. The earthy scent of the forest filled her lungs and she breathed it in, the pain in her shoulder settling back to a dull throb.

A car engine…no…several car engines roared up the gravel road. Cordelia? Already? *Shit, shit, shit.*

Annabelle stumbled to her feet, flattened herself against the rough timber of the cabin and inched her way forward. Taking a deep breath, she peered around the corner. Her mouth dropped open. Four familiar cars pulled up in a scattering of gravel, and out poured members of her coven — Isobella, Aunt Marjory, her mom and her stepdad, Emmanuel, Roger, the Milners and the Tisdales. The cavalry had come. How had they known where to find her?

A big black wolf with green eyes leaped out of the first car, its hackles standing on end and its lips curled back in a snarl revealing vicious-looking canines.

Stefanie?

Holy crap. The woman…wolf…was *huge*.

The front door banged against the side of the cabin, flung open from inside, and Annabelle pulled her head back. The porch creaked. Annabelle risked another peek. Scarface, with a mean looking sawn-off shotgun in his hands, walked to the edge of the rickety porch.

Aunt Marjory stepped forward, no hint of fear on her face. "Release my niece."

Annabelle grinned. Oh, yeah. Her great aunt was a badass in high heels and designer suits.

"Or?" sneered Scarface.

Aunt Marjory raised one perfectly shaped eyebrow. "Or you die?"

Scarface chuckled. "*Madam*, it iz we...'ow you Americans say...who 'old all ze cards, no?"

A blur of black fur burst from the shadows of the forest, hurtled toward the porch and slammed into Scarface. It knocked him to the ground. Annabelle jumped back. Another wolf? Her heart lurched into her throat. Gabriel? No, it couldn't be. The wolf snarled and snapped at Scarface, huge canines finding purchase. Scarface bellowed, and the shotgun went off. Birds screeched and took flight. Annabelle slapped her hand over her mouth, smothering a scream. Then wolf and man went rolling across the clearing, a confusing mass of growling fur and grunting man.

The door banged open again, and two more men appeared on the porch. Too late. The witches were already filling the air with the chanting of spells and the electric charge of magic. In mere moments, the coven had the men bound and on the ground. Where was Dutton?

Annabelle stumbled forward. Down the hill, the wolf and Scarface fought on. The wolf lunged for Scarface's throat. The Frenchman threw up his arm, blocking the blow, but the wolf latched on, digging his teeth in and shaking his head. Scarface screamed.

Hackles raised and ready to pounce, should Scarface get the upper hand, was the wolf Annabelle pegged as Stefanie. In front, the witches were pounding up the steps of the cabin. Annabelle had to warn Aunt Marjory. Dutton could be lying in wait. Or he could have already fled like the coward he was.

A muscled arm caught her about the throat and reefed her back against a hard chest. A glint of silver flashed near her face, and then the steely point jabbed ever so slightly into her neck. Annabelle stilled.

"Well, well, well. Look what I've found. Where do you think you're going, Annabee?"

Dutton. Her mind raced.

"You think you're so clever escaping through the chimney. But I still have your blood. And now I have you. Let's take a little walk in the forest, shall we? Just you and me. And you won't make a sound, or I will spell your mouth shut."

He really *was* an idiot. Did he think Stefanie couldn't track her? Maybe he'd called in backup. He could've, should've, used magic on her while she was unaware of his presence. But he was so confident he had the upper hand. That he could stop her from reciting any spell. That magic was her only means of defense. Or that a knife at her throat would stop her from fighting any way she could. Did he think, with all the turmoil in their coven, and the prospect she might soon be taking a trip to Medieval Europe, she'd not started taking defense classes?

"I don't think so, Dutton. I'm not going anywhere with you."

Before the certainty in her voice gave her away, Annabelle grabbed hold of his forearm and cocked her right hip and shoulder up. She ducked beneath his arm, controlling his forearm and the knife, wrenching it down away from her face as her instructor had taught her. She slipped out from beneath him, but kept her body close, and with all the strength she could muster with her injured shoulder, she plunged the knife into his side. It all happened so fast, Dutton didn't seem to realize she'd stabbed *him*. With his own knife. That would teach him to underestimate her.

Dutton struggled, trying to use his height advantage and his gym body to regain the upper hand.

Annabelle growled and plunged the knife in again. "That's for Gabriel."

This time Dutton gasped and doubled over.

Annabelle slipped her hand down to his wrist and twisted, as she'd practiced in class. Dutton loosened his grip. The knife was now in her hands. She stepped back. With a bellow, Dutton lunged. Annabelle high-kicked him in the face and then her mom, her stepdad and Isobella were there, chanting a spell. Dutton dropped like a stone.

Chapter Twenty

The knife slipped from Annabelle's nerveless fingers. A tremor, starting at her bloody hand, worked its way through her body and all the way down to her toes. Her poor shoulder throbbed worse than ever.

Her mom rushed over and enfolded her in a hug. "Annabelle. Thank the Lord you're okay."

Her stepdad followed, then Isobella, Annabelle's shoulder protesting.

"If it wasn't for that wolf shifter of yours," said her mother, "we might never have found you."

Her wolf shifter? Annabelle pulled away from her family. "Gabriel?"

"Yes."

Her mom pointed at the big black wolf standing over the body of Scarface. Red stained the wolf's muzzle, and Scarface's throat was bloody and torn.

Annabelle took a step towards the wolf. *Gabriel?* He was even bigger than Stefanie. His furry head turned her way, his dark eyes boring into her. A strong musky scent, tinged with something familiar, hung heavy in the air. She could almost taste it. Taste him.

The wolf's fur rippled, bones popped, and fur receded. His big body contorted as paws turned to hands and feet, and his snout shrunk into a human nose. Then he was upright and standing before her.

"Gabriel. Dutton told me... I thought you were..." A sob tore from her throat, and she stumbled toward him. She halted as she got a clear look at him. "Oh, my God. Look at you."

Dark purple bruises covered his body from his left shoulder, across his chest and down past his hip. From the crash? Tears filled her eyes and her hand hovered over one of the larger ones.

He took hold of her hand. "I'm okay, *bebe*. I'm healing." Then he enfolded her in his arms. "I told you I wasn't going to leave you, and I meant it."

She pulled away and stared up at him. "How? I mean... There's no way you could have walked away from that crash." Her fingers traced one of his bruises.

Gabriel caught the bottle of water Stefanie tossed him, and he washed the blood from his face. "I didn't. They took me away in an ambulance and I spent two days in hospital."

"Two days... But I..." She glanced over her shoulder at the cabin. "I've not been here a day yet. Have I?"

"I used the spell. From the grimoire."

"You...you found the grimoire?"

He grinned. "I stole it from Rarity. I broke your ward."

Annabelle winced.

"*Oui.* It didn't tickle." He tossed the water bottle aside and cupped her face in his big hands. "But I would do it all again in a heartbeat. For you, Annabelle."

He dropped his lips to hers, and with a sigh, Annabelle melted into him. He swiped his tongue along the seam of her lips and she opened for him. He was alive. He was here. He'd broken her ward and pushed his bruised and battered body through time to get to her.

"Mmm-hmm."

Annabelle surfaced, and Gabriel glared at their intruder, Stefanie, once again in human form and fully clothed.

Stef tossed Gabriel his shirt, jacket and jeans. "I'm sure Annabelle loves your crown jewels, but the rest of us could do without seeing them. Or your naked ass."

Annabelle clapped her hands to her mouth. "Oh, my God. I didn't even think. You must be freezing."

Gabriel stepped into his jeans. "Wolf shifter, *bebe*, remember? Our temperatures run hotter."

Annabelle took in his taut, naked ass before he covered it up with denim. *That they did.*

Aunt Marjory strode over, no more hindered by her heels on the gravel than if she were walking on Italian palazzo tiles. "This reeks of Cordelia."

"Oh, she was involved all right." Annabelle hugged her arms around her body, holding herself together, her eyes straying to Gabriel as he dressed. She still couldn't believe he was alive, and had risked everything to save her. "Cordelia had Dutton take my blood. They had plans to turn me into a puppet bride for Dutton using Cordelia's magic." She nodded at the cabin. "They were her wards on the basement. When I couldn't break through them, I started searching for some other way to escape. How long the Kings have owned this place is anyone's guess, but they either didn't know about the broken chimney, or they didn't think I'd find it." Annabelle sighed. "To be honest, I wasn't expecting anyone to find me. I thought..." She turned to Gabriel. "I thought you were dead. How could anyone, even a shifter, survive a hit like that?"

He pulled her close, and she rested her head on his chest. "It would take more than that to keep me from you, *mon amour*."

Aunt Marjory crossed her arms, tapping her sleeve with a manicured fingernail. "Would this have something to do with what makes you different from the local shifters, Gabriel?"

"It does, but..."

Annabelle looked up at him. Was he still going to keep her out? After all that had happened?

He brushed a strand of hair off her face. "There are things I'm only permitted to share with Annabelle. Anything else must come from Maxime d'Louncrais, our alpha. Some secrets are best kept that way."

Aunt Marjory nodded. "I trust Annabelle to consider the coven's interest in this and do what is best for all of us."

Roger joined them. "Good to see you're okay, kiddo. We've taken the three survivors into custody. Dutton will survive. He's getting medical care now. Not that he deserves it, mind you. We've buried the other one. Not sure what three Frenchmen have to do with all this..."

"I'll fill Annabelle in on that, too," said Gabriel.

Aunt Marjory nodded. "Very well. Roger, call a meeting of the coven. We'll deal with these men in-house. And Cordelia. Send a team to collect her and bring her before the coven."

Roger's grin was wicked. "With pleasure."

"Annabelle, get your mom to do a healing spell on that shoulder of yours. Then take Isobella and your parents and search the house for those vials of blood. Destroy them."

The High Priestess turned to Gabriel. "If I heard correctly, you used that spell to find Annabelle. You had best get going back to the future. We really do not know what will happen if you run into yourself. Let's not ruin a good outcome by pushing the limits and finding out the ramifications are disastrous."

"*Oui.*" He turned to her. "When you're done here, *mon amour*, go with Stef back to the Ritz-Carlton. I'll meet you there." He looked over her shoulder. "And bring Isobella with you. There are some things she needs to hear, too."

Annabelle scrunched up her face. *Isobella? Why?*

Stef smirked and patted her on the arm. "Don't worry, Annabelle. After we've had a talk, Isobella and I will disappear. Apparently, Lenni's does amazing pizzas. Isobella and I have plans to watch the movie you Americans call *Die Hard* and continue our debate over whether it's a Christmas movie."

Her aunt, Stef and her family moved away to go about their respective tasks.

Isobella jerked her head to the cabin. "I'll, um, see you inside."

Then she was alone with Gabriel.

"I'm sorry we—"

"I should never have left you in—"

Annabelle stared at her shoe as she scuffed at the dirt with her toe. "You first."

"I promise I will explain everything, Annabelle. Why I left you in Paris, everything. I promise."

She nodded. "Okay. You'd better. I'll be waiting."

Annabelle stood on her tiptoes and kissed him on the lips, then turned and walked toward the house. Lying in that basement, believing him to be dead, she'd have given everything to go back to before the crash. To tell him she loved him. Had always loved him. But he'd left her in Paris, and she needed to know why. She needed answers to a lot of questions. Then, and only then, would she tell him she'd already forgiven him.

Chapter Twenty-One

Gabriel landed with a thump on the forest floor, having forced his aching body through a tear in the fabric of time once more. *Putain*, his body hurt, but his heart no longer squeezed in his chest. Annabelle was alive and safe. He rolled onto his back and stared up at the night sky, a grin teasing the corners of his mouth. His woman was strong. She'd gotten herself out of that basement all by herself. And she'd taken down Dutton with the *fils de pute's* own knife. What an amazing woman. Annabelle, his mate. It was time to tell her everything. It was time to claim her and make her one of them.

He sent a text to Stefanie, telling her he was on his way. Then he called for an Uber. It took him three attempts to get one to meet him at the entrance of Muir Woods. The monument had closed at five. It was now eleven. No one wanted to come out to the woods. And for a foreigner, no less. Not at this time of night. He'd recited the spell around midday, spent perhaps three hours at most in the past, but he'd returned eleven hours later. It was a good thing Isobella wouldn't be coming back. Who knew how inaccurate the spell would be if someone went *that* far back in time.

A light rain was falling as he paid the Uber driver and entered the hotel. Would Annabelle be awake and waiting for him? Would she still be in his suite? He leaned against the elevator wall. *L'enfer*, he was tired, and he needed a shower. But first, Annabelle and Isobella needed to know the truth. Then he thought he might sleep for a week. As long as Annabelle was curled up against his side, he would be a happy man. And wolf.

If she'd have him. He'd thought he'd seen something in her expression as he'd held her in his arms by the cabin in the forest. A softening of her anger toward him. But he had a lot of explaining to do, and she could well reject him as her mate. It didn't happen often, but it did happen. It'd happened to Maxime. Would Annabelle accept him? Or would she doom him to long nights of melancholy drinking with Maxime? Two lone wolves bereft of their mates.

He stepped through the vestibule and into the penthouse apartment. Annabelle stood by the floor-to-ceiling windows, looking out across the San Francisco night skyline. The memory of her naked, her hands pressed against the glass as he'd taken her from behind, flashed through his mind. His cock instantly rose to the occasion. *Oui*, he wanted to do that again. Soon. Not now. Not with Isobella sitting on the sofa, concern in her dark eyes. Concern for him or Annabelle? Or for her role in this?

"About time." Annabelle turned to face him, her arms folded across her chest. "You have a lot of explaining to do, Gabriel."

"*Oui*. Whatever you need to know, *ma chérie*."

She took a few steps toward him, but not close enough for him to draw her into his arms. She wasn't going to make this easy for him.

"Who was that man with Dutton? Scarface?" she demanded.

Stef sauntered in from the kitchen, handed him a glass of whiskey and gave him a look that said he was on his own with this one.

He took a large swig, letting it burn down the back of his throat. "His name was Gerard Boucher. He belonged to a fanatical group in France whose origins date back to the tenth century. They follow the writings of Eveque Faucher. They believe that any supernatural being like me, like you, are evil, and they dedicate their lives to hunting and destroying them. Because of Faucher's experience with my ancestors, he had a particular fixation with the Langeais wolves. The Faucherians have continued with his obsession."

Annabelle screwed up her nose. "The Faucherians? They call themselves the *Faucherians*?"

Stef snorted. "A stupid name for stupid people."

"Wait a minute." Annabelle frowned. "That doesn't make any sense. If he believed supernatural beings to be evil, if these *Faucherians* believe the same, why would they work with a witch? With Dutton?"

"I don't know. Perhaps it suited them to for the moment."

"That's hypocritical."

Gabriel took another sip of whiskey. "I said they were dedicated, not that they were intelligent. Or sane. But it is concerning. Faucher wasn't the only enemy my ancestors faced. There was a witch, a time-traveling witch named Cordelia."

Annabelle's eyebrows shot up. "Cordelia. As in, Cordelia King?"

"I think so. Isobella says she has two different colored eyes.

Annabelle nodded. "She does. Heterochromia. It's a genetic mutation.

"Then she fits the description."

Annabelle flicked open the grimoire on the coffee table, turning page after page. "Do you think—"

"Yes."

Annabelle contemplated the book of spells. "That's pretty bad news for our coven. I'll have to inform Aunt Marjory. Maybe show her the grimoire." She shut the book. "What are we going to do with this thing when we've finished with it?

"I've spoken to Maxime, our alpha," said Stef. "He wants Alain to look at it. He's a wolf witch in our pack, and he's a newly elected member of the Council of Witches."

Gabriel snapped his gaze to Stef. "They elected *Alain* to the council? After what happened last year? How the hell did that happen? Didn't they have *any* other candidates?"

Stef held up her hands. "Don't ask me."

"Let's get back to these Faucherians." Annabelle's gaze flicked between him and Stef. "These people have been hunting your pack since the tenth century. And they followed you here. Did they have anything to do with why you left me in Paris?"

His woman was smart.

"They were a big part of the reason. Twenty-five years ago, they attacked and killed our alpha and his mate. Stefanie and Maxime's parents. With them at the time was their youngest daughter, Nathalie. Three years ago, a woman claiming to be her surfaced in Langeais. Everything pointed to her being who she claimed to be, but she wasn't the first to make that claim. Then the Faucherians got involved. She didn't know it, but they were using her as bait. If she really was Nathalie d'Louncrais, we couldn't lose her again. I had to go."

"Gabriel is essentially our head of security," said Stef. "He takes his job very seriously. Perhaps a little too seriously."

Gabriel shot Stef a look. "Thanks, Stef."

She shrugged. "Well, you could have told Annabelle then, and we wouldn't be here now."

Gabriel gritted his teeth. "She wasn't ready."

Annabelle held out her hands. "Ready for what? To know you were a shifter?"

Gabriel sighed. "I didn't know you were a witch. And we're not like other shifters, Annabelle."

"So you keep saying, but what does that mean? You've already told me you can't impregnate a human. Oh." Her face fell. "That's it, isn't it? You won't mate me because I can't provide you with pups."

The hurt brimming in her eyes broke his heart.

"Is that what you needed to tell me?" Her voice rose an octave, and she hugged herself tight. "You say you won't leave me, so…what? I'm to become some sort of *mistress*? Well, I have news for you, Gabriel Montagne." Now her finger was out, and she was shaking it at him, her blue eyes stormy. "I"—she poked herself in the chest—"I am *no one's* mistress."

He crossed the room in quick strides. How had this all gone so wrong so fast? He gathered her in his arms despite her protests. She writhed against him, which did nothing to help his already hard cock at all.

"Annabelle, Belle, you *are* my mate. And the *only* woman for me."

She stopped struggling. "But… What about…"

He planted a kiss on the bridge of her nose. "Belle, I cannot get a human pregnant, but I also said the Langeais wolves differ from other wolves. That we are *true* werewolves."

She stared up at him, confusion written across her face.

"My bite, my claim, will make you mine, but it will also make you one of us."

Her eyes widened. "One of — " She searched his face. "You can turn humans into werewolves?"

He smiled down at her. "Yes, Annabelle, we can. If you'll let me, if you consent to be my mate, I'd like very much to turn you."

Chapter Twenty-Two

Annabelle stared up at Gabriel. *I am his mate?*

"Are you saying...? Are we...? If you turn me into...?"

"You'll be like me. Or more precisely, like my cousin Alain. He's a wolf witch. It'll take some training, but you'll be both a practicing witch and a werewolf. Most importantly, you'll be mine."

That last word had a hint of a growl.

"And you'll be mine, too, right?"

He broke into a grin. "Forever, *bebe*. Forever. Are you saying yes?"

Annabelle's heart flip-flopped around in her chest. She really liked the sound of that. Her and Gabriel together. Finally. Would he move to the States? Would she move to Paris? She couldn't leave the coven. Not now. Maybe not ever. Would he be prepared to leave his pack? They'd never had any of these conversations. He'd left too soon in Paris. He hadn't known she was a witch. She hadn't known he was a shifter.

"You're thinking really hard there, *mon amour*."

"It's just there's so many details—"

The implications were...*huge*. For her, for them, for the coven and for her mission. The mission...

He pressed a finger to her lips. "Belle, I would never ask you to leave your coven. I know you are to take over from Marjory. Stef is right. I take my job too seriously. If Paris taught me anything, it's that I need to learn to delegate. My fellow wolves have been itching to prove themselves. I can do most of my job from here."

Tears pricked her eyes. He would move away from his pack for her? "Yes." She wrapped her arms around his neck. "Yes, Gabriel Montagne, make me your mate." He picked her up and swung her around, beaming, and she laughed at his exuberance. "Of course, we'll have to postpone the mission for a bit, I suppose, until I'm properly trained," she said when her feet were back on the floor.

His smile disappeared.

She pulled out of his arms. "Oh no, Gabriel. Just because I've agreed to be your mate doesn't mean you can start that overprotective shifter bullshit. Don't forget, I was the one who got myself out of that basement. *I* was the one who took down Dutton."

"Annabelle—"

"No. If you have a problem with me taking on this mission, you can come with me. You've used the spell now. You know what to expect."

"Annabelle—"

"Two of us will be better than one. We'll have a better chance of taking out Faucher. That's the only concession I'm willing to make."

"Annabelle, stop. That's not what this is about." He shared a glance with Stef, then they both looked at Isobella. "Isobella is the one who must go."

Isobella gasped. "Me?" She jumped to her feet. "I can't go, I..."

"We know you're sick, Isobella," said Stef.

Annabelle rounded on Isobella. "You're sick? How? When? Why didn't you tell me?"

Isobella hugged herself. "I... I've only just found out. I was going to tell you all—Dad, Mom, the High Priestess." She took a shaky breath. "I'm dying."

"Well, we'll use a healing spell. We'll get the whole coven involved—minus the Kings, of course."

Isobella stared at her with sad eyes. "Annabelle, this is not a sore shoulder that a simple spell, no matter how many people are chanting it, will heal. I have ovarian cancer. Stage four."

"What about chemo? There has to be something." She couldn't lose Isobella. She was the only sibling she had. And she hadn't had her sister nearly long enough to suit her.

Gabriel cupped her face. "There is something, but it means Isobella going on this mission."

Annabelle pushed him away. "Going on this mission will kill her. For sure. There's no medical intervention, no treatment for cancer in the tenth century, Gabriel. They barely have sanitation or personal hygiene." Annabelle stamped her foot on the ground. "She's not going."

"What something?" piped up Isobella. "Stef? Gabriel? You said there was something that could treat me. What is it?"

Gabriel sighed. "I can't tell you that, Isobella. I'm sorry. If I do, it might change what you do and it will never come to be. What I can tell you is that you survive and live a long life. In the tenth century."

Annabelle glared at Gabriel. "How do you even know that?"

"Because, Belle, Isobella going back, taking on this mission to eradicate Faucher, changes everything. This is the real reason we came. To ensure Isobella does what she is supposed to do. If she does not... The future as we know it will be different. How different?" He shrugged. "Perhaps the Langeais wolves no longer exist." Gabriel caressed her cheek. "Perhaps, Belle, you and I will never meet. Who knows what effect it will have."

Isobella sat down heavily on the couch. "Are you certain, without a doubt, that I survive?"

"Yes," both Gabriel and Stef answered.

Isobella stared out of the window at the glowing lights of the San Francisco skyline. "I'll go."

"What? No. Just no." Annabelle glared at the three of them. "Are you crazy, Isobella? Are you *all* crazy? Gabriel, you've used the spell. You know what it feels like. How much it hurts. Like your body is being folded in half and squeezed through a rift in the fabric of time so small you don't think it's possible to fit through, but you do. Isobella is sick, and you want to put her through that?"

There was another way. Annabelle turned to look at her mate. At Stef. Shifters both. Impervious to disease and illness. Not much could kill a shifter. Not even cancer. And both with the ability to turn humans. "You can save her, Gabriel. Right here. Right now. Or you, Stefanie. All you have to do is turn her. Right?"

Stef shook her head. "That's not advisable."

"And why not?"

Gabriel gripped her shoulders and turned her to face him. "Believe me, Belle, I would if I could. If we change even one thing, we risk changing everything. Isobella has to go back as she is. Besides, our alpha must sanction all turnings, and Maxime will never agree to it. I'm sorry, Isobella. It's the only way."

"I'll go," Isobella said, more firmly this time.

Annabelle pulled away from Gabriel and went to her sister. "Isobella, you don't have to do this. I can…" She glanced between Gabriel and Stef, their faces masks of resolve. Neither one of them would turn Isobella. No matter what she said, they'd made up their minds. It stood to reason none of their pack would turn her, either. But she could. Once Gabriel turned her. *Then*, maybe, she'd be okay with Isobella going back in time to do whatever it was she was supposed to do.

"I know what you're thinking, Annabelle," growled Gabriel. "Maxime won't allow it."

Annabelle snorted. She wasn't going to let this Maxime tell her she couldn't save her sister.

"You'll need time to learn to control your wolf, Annabelle," said Stef. "How much time is anyone's guess. It'll depend on how fast you learn. Will Isobella have enough time to wait for you?"

With Isobella's life on the line, Annabelle would be a motivated student.

"No, Annabelle." Gabriel shook his head. "If this is what you intend to do, you leave me no choice. I won't claim you until Isobella has used the spell."

From the set of his jaw, Gabriel would stand by his words. Then Isobella would die anyway.

"It's okay, Annabelle," said Isobella. "Really. I would never want to come between you and Gabriel. I'll go."

"But…"

Isobella gave her a wan smile. "I have a thirty-one percent chance of living maybe another five years *if* I have chemo and surgery. Thirty-one percent, Annabelle. Five years, and that's with invasive surgery and months of debilitating chemotherapy. Forget a long and happy life. Forget having a family." She stared past Annabelle to Gabriel and Stef. "They're offering me the chance for both. What choice would *you* make?"

Chapter Twenty-Three

Annabelle's shoulders dropped, and the fight seemed to go out of her. In four quick steps, he was behind her, gently stroking her shoulders.

She leaned back into him, and he nuzzled the top of her head. "It's late. It's been a hectic and traumatic few days. Why don't we all get some sleep and talk about this again in the morning?"

"There's nothing to talk about. I'm going." Isobella took Annabelle's hand. "You know this is the best option. I can do this, Annabelle."

Determination flashed in Isobella's eyes, and for a moment, Gabriel saw the woman who would not only survive in the tenth century, but would thrive.

"But I am tired." Isobella dropped Annabelle's hand, picked up her purse and slung it over her shoulder. "Stef, would you mind taking me home? And, uh, I'm guessing Annabelle's bed will be free tonight if you want to crash at our place." She jerked her head toward him and Annabelle. "I imagine these two have a bit of catching up to do."

"Of course, Isobella," said Stef. "And yes, the offer of a bed is much appreciated. These two are likely to be noisy, and my poor ears and refined sensibilities aren't up for listening to that."

With her parting shot and a wink, Stef followed Isobella, leaving them alone in the penthouse.

Annabelle turned in his arms and leaned her head against his chest.

"Is she really going to be okay, Gabriel?"

"*Oui.* I promise." He dropped a kiss on her head. "I couldn't say anything more in front of Isobella, but I don't want to keep anything from you. Not anymore. You deserve to know the truth. If Isobella is half as smart as you, she'll have a good idea of what's going to happen."

Annabelle jerked her head back to look at him. "Someone's going to turn her? A werewolf in the tenth century?"

Gabriel grinned. "*Oui.*"

"And you know who it is, don't you?"

Gabriel nodded. "Neither I, nor my brothers, would exist if it were not for Isobella. She's my many times great-great-grandmother."

Annabelle gaped at him, her mouth working like a fish out of water. "Isobella is your *ancestor?*"

"Isobella is going to survive, Annabelle. I'm here, aren't I? I'm living proof she's going to be more than okay."

She wrapped her arms around his waist and snuggled deeper. It was so good to have her in his arms again. Right where she belonged.

"Trust me, Annabelle. It will all work out exactly as it's meant to."

"I hope so."

He held her close, the events of today still fresh in his mind. If he never time traveled again, it would be too soon.

"So, what happens now?" She gazed up at him, wariness in her blue eyes. "With us, I mean? Do you bite me and…" She gave him a nervous smile. "I'm not sure how this is supposed to work."

Gabriel chuckled. "Ever the impatient one." He cupped her face. "All in good time, *bebe*. Let's not rush things." He pressed a finger to her lips. "Now, before you start fretting, I am going to turn you, that I promise. And soon. But a turning is not something you want to rush. We'll need medical supplies and time."

"Medical supplies?" she squeaked around his finger.

"The turning is painful. I'll keep you sedated for the three days you'll need, then—"

"*Three* days?"

"Three days," he affirmed. "Then you'll need perhaps three months, maybe more, of training. Three months where we'll need space and privacy so you don't accidentally shift and reveal yourself in the middle of downtown San Francisco."

"Oh."

Her disappointment was a balm to his chaotic emotions. She wanted the turning as much as he did. But it would not be tonight, no matter how much his wolf called for it. Or how much his canines threatened to punch through his gums at the thought of sinking into the soft curve of her neck. He needed to rest and to be in prime condition before she began her turning. Annabelle as a witch was a handful. As a wolf witch, she would test all his reserves. Reserves he did not have right now.

"Tonight, I need a nice hot shower and then to sleep in a soft bed with the woman I love in my arms."

At his declaration of his feelings, her pretty mouth parted on a gasp, and his cock surged. Okay, maybe not only a shower and sleep.

A slow smile spread across Annabelle's lips, and he caught the mischievous glint in her eyes. She took his hand and led him up the floating staircase and into the master suite bathroom. She turned and slipped off her jacket, dropped it to the floor and toed off her shoes. With a tug on her blouse, she pulled it out from the waistband of her jeans and unbuttoned it, one slow button at a time.

Gabriel swallowed. Moonlight bathed the room, giving everything — the lava stone tiles, the soaking tub, the large shower, the double vanities, Annabelle — a bluish cast, like a black and white film effect. With his enhanced vision, the subtle shadows of her collarbones, the curve of her breasts, the dampness of her lower lip after she'd run her tongue across it were clear to him. Did he scoop her up now and rip the rest of her clothes off? Or did he wait, watch and enjoy the slow reveal of her creamy breasts cupped in white lace?

Her blouse joined her jacket, then she popped the button on her jeans. Gabriel was torn. The slow slide of her zipper echoed loud in his ears with the promise of sex. Annabelle's jeans joined her blouse, leaving her in two pieces of white lace. The sweet and tantalizing scent of her arousal bloomed and hit him harder than the Mack truck from their crash.

Putain, she was beautiful. For a moment, he was too stunned to move. Then a slow smile spread across his lips. Quid pro quo, *bebe*.

Gabriel ditched his jacket, grasped the back of his shirt and pulled it over his head, tossing it aside. He snapped the button on his jeans. Her gaze blazed a trail across his abdomen, and her breathing hitched. He slid his zipper down with slow deliberation. Her heart beat a staccato rhythm, louder than a bass drum to his sensitive ears. Then he kicked off his boots, peeled off his socks and shucked his jeans. He stood naked before her, legs spread and his cock granite hard and already leaking pre-cum.

"You're not naked yet, Annabelle." His words were barely more than a growl.

Her trembling hands reached behind her back, undid the clasp and her *soutien-gorge* slid to the floor, revealing rosy nipples peaked and ready for his touch. Her white lace panties, she slid down over her hips, the hint of dampness glistening on the fabric and on the fine blonde hair at the crutch of her thighs.

Gabriel breathed her in, and a throaty rumble reverberated through his chest. There was no finer perfume in all of this world than the scent of his mate aroused. He would never tire of it.

She backed away from him and slipped into the large, glass-walled shower, the San Francisco night skyline visible behind her. Gabriel stepped in after her as she turned on the taps and adjusted the water. He slid his hands around her waist as the water sluiced over them both. With soap in hand, she turned in his arms, swiveled them around until he was under the spray and began a slow, sensuous, slippery exploration of his body, lathering his skin and washing him down as she went. His arms, his shoulders, his pecs, sliding her petite hands across his stomach.

Annabelle ducked behind him, washing his back, caressing his spine, cupping his ass cheeks and rubbing down his legs setting every nerve ending on fire. Never had he experienced such devotion, such tenderness.

His heart swelled, and so did his cock. He didn't think he'd ever been this hard for a woman, not even Annabelle, in his entire life.

She stepped in front of him, her hands reaching for his groin and gently soaping up his balls. He threw his head back, letting the water wash over him. Then she took his cock in hand, sliding her hands along his length. Another growl rumbled up in his chest and her hand faltered.

"Keep going like that and this will be all over in a matter of seconds."

She kept going.

No. He was not some pimply youth, thinking only of his own pleasure. He gently eased her hands away and grabbed the soap. His turn.

Gabriel started at the curve of her throat, gentling massaging the tension from her shoulders, down her arms to her fingertips. More soap suds frothed as he cupped her breasts, teasing her pert nipples until a low moan slipped from her lips. His hands roamed, rediscovering her body—the curves and shallows, the mole on the inside of her hip, the tender spot on her inner thigh, the way her legs shook when he rubbed at the back of her knees, the plumpness of her ass and the heat of her slippery folds.

A fierceness washed over him. He'd nearly lost her. For good. Who knew what would've become of her had Dutton's plan succeeded. He never wanted to let her out of his sight again, though Annabelle would chafe at such restrictions. They'd argue about it, and she would rightly claim she could take care of herself, like she had with Dutton, but the beast in him would always be protective of her. Three long years without her had been pure hell.

Three long years without being able to cup her pussy, slide his fingers inside her and feel her clench around him. To live without her sweet body pressed against him. Without hearing her little noises of pleasure—her moans and gasps as he hit her sweet spot. Or the fluttering of her hands about his neck, urging him on.

"Gabriel," she breathed, a plea and exhortation for more.

He took her mouth in his, delving deep with his tongue, as he eased two fingers inside her. A leisurely seduction, unlike the savage need of their fucking a few nights previous. *Putain*, he'd missed this.

She protested when he slid his fingers out, but her complaints faded into a moan as he lifted her, wrapped her legs around his hips and slowly, inexorably seated her down the length of his cock. Planting his feet wide for stability on the wet floor, he pressed her back against the tiles and began a slide and grind with his hips, setting up a measured pace as if he had all the time in the world. Wanting to prolong this for as long as he could.

L'enfer, he did. The slippery slide of the wet bodies, the warm water on their heated skin, her soft whimpers and the silken grip of her pussy around his cock were all the heaven he needed. Like all his Christmases had come at once. Three years of hell, washed away with the water swirling the drain.

Her head dropped into the crook of his neck, and her thighs squeezed around his hips. "Yes, yes, yes. Don't stop, Gabriel," she huffed out. "Whatever you do, don't stop."

"I've got you, Belle." He would never stop. Fucking her. Loving her. Not for the rest of his long life. He plunged deep, bottoming out, and she let out a hoarse cry, clamping her blunt teeth on his shoulder. Pleasure ripped up his spine, tightened his balls and his whole body stiffened. He thrust in one last time, then roared his release as she milked his seed and sucked him dry.

He slumped against her, his chest heaving. "Mine," he growled into her wet hair.

She unlatched her teeth from his shoulder. "Yours," she whispered against his skin. "I love you. I don't think...I ever stopped," she said, between breaths. "When you left...I looked for you. In Paris."

Gabriel held her tight, the warm water from the shower no match for the warmth in his chest as her words washed over him.

"I looked for you too, Belle, but you were gone."

She snuggled into his chest. "I stayed for a month. Hoping you'd return. But you never called, or texted. Nothing. I didn't think you were coming back. I couldn't stay in Paris any longer. It wasn't the same without you." Her voice warbled a little. "We might never have reconnected had your pack not sent you to our coven."

"Ah, *bebe*, I was still looking for you. I was always going to come for you one day."

She raised her gaze, water plastering her hair to her head. "You were?"

Then the water turned cold and she squealed. Laughing, he flicked it off and carried her into the bedroom.

"I'm all wet!" she shrieked as he tossed her onto the bed.

"I hope so," he said, grinning, as he followed her down onto the sheets. They had a lot of years to make up for. She was in his arms again, finally, and Gabriel was not planning on wasting a single moment.

Chapter Twenty-Four

Two days later
Christmas Eve

Isobella held her breath as the shocked silence continued. Her stepmom's face had paled and concern shimmered in her father's eyes, the turkey, stuffing and roast vegetables forgotten. The Christmas tree lights winked on and off, cycling through the colors, tinging the room with first red, then yellow, then blue, then green. No one moved or spoke, staring at her like she'd grown another head. Or sprouted horns.

Isobella set her fork down on her plate with a clang. "I can do this. I know I can."

The High Priestess, Aunt Marjory, smiled at her. "Of course you can, Isobella. I trust Annabelle's judgment. If she didn't think you capable of taking on the mission to the tenth century, she wouldn't have recommended you. Neither would the Langeais wolves."

Her father frowned. "It's not that we don't think you capable, *mija*, but—"

"Are you sure you want to do this?" interrupted her stepmom. "It is understandable, after what happened with…" She blushed and cleared her throat. "Of course you're looking for a new adventure, something to sink your teeth into, but…"

"This has nothing to do with my breakup with Douglas. This is about me. I *want* to do this."

Leaving her father was going to break her heart, and her father's, but Gabriel and Annabelle would be here to tell him the truth. To give him some comfort. If the choice were between her not going and dying, and going and surviving in the tenth century, her father would make the same choice she had. All she had to do was keep her illness a secret until she left. If they knew, they'd all try to stop her.

* * * *

Cordelia's gnarled fingers gripped her knitting needles. Knit one, purl one, knit one, purl one. Knitting calmed her, and she needed a lot of calm after the mess Dutton had made of things. Stupid fool had nearly gotten himself killed by that slip of a girl, Annabelle. If he hadn't been so besotted with the idea of having the pretty blonde witch in his bed, they might not be in this position. He'd underestimated her. Typical. Men always underestimated women. And sadly, women overestimated men. As she had with that fool son of hers.

Her needles clacked together with a vicious snap. She should never have trusted him after he got himself cast off the d'Louncrais estate back in the tenth century. He'd had one job. Ingratiate himself with the alpha of the Langeais wolves—Jacques d'Louncrais—and he'd failed. She should never have trusted him with her grimoire. She should have gone back for it, risked another trip to the tenth century to ensure it was safe. Even after what had happened.

Where else would Annabelle have gotten a time-traveling spell if not from her grimoire? Cordelia snorted. Not from a French illuminated manuscript, as she claimed. It was a shame Roger had found the listening devices in Marjory's office. The interesting conversations she'd still be privy to if they hadn't.

She rocked back and forth in her chair, her needles clicking around green and red wool as she knitted a Christmas sweater for Douglas, the new paramour of one of her great nieces. All was not lost. The coven hadn't found her. And they were unlikely to. Nor would the Langeais wolves. She had several properties to hide out in, none of them connected to her via any paper or digital trail. And she had her contingency plan. It would keep those clever Montagne twins busy unraveling all her false trails.

The death of Gerard Boucher, while an inconvenient situation, had not severed her connection with the Faucherians. She made a gurgling sound in the back of her throat. What a stupid name for an organization, but one couldn't expect too much from zealots.

She paused in her knitting and rested her gnarled hands in her lap. For too long she'd been on the losing end of her skirmishes with the Langeais wolves. Not this time. She'd get her grimoire back, she'd take over the coven, and then she'd destroy those French werewolves. Here, now, or in the tenth century, she didn't care which. With the knowledge and resources of the Faucherians, she could not fail.

* * * *

Alain d'Louncrais scrolled through the images on his phone, the blood in his veins icier than the frosted air beyond his hotel window. Spells, each one darker than the first, sent to him by Gabriel.

The bedsheets rustled behind him. "Come back to bed, Alain."

He eyed the pretty, naked witch in his bed, her dark hair spread across the pale sheets. "In a minute, *ma chérie.*"

She pouted. "We're supposed to be celebrating your election to the witch's council." She let the sheet slip down, revealing one full breast and a dark, pert nipple. "Come celebrate with me."

Alain knew who the grimoire had belonged to, who'd written it. She'd come for it, sooner or later, but there was nothing he could do about any of it tonight.

He smiled and set aside his phone. "What did you have in mind, *ma chérie?*"

Alain climbed back into bed and pushed the grimoire from his thoughts. For now.

* * * *

Pierre leaned back on the sofa, *Joyeux Noel* playing on the television. "You have outdone yourself this year, Louis. I don't think I could eat another bite."

His twin, Louis, slumped next to him. "Me either."

Pierre's phone pinged, and he dragged himself up to check it. "Typical. It's Christmas Eve and Maxime's still working."

Louis groaned. "Wasn't the Christmas tree in his office enough of a hint?"

"I guess not." Pierre frowned at the message on his phone. He turned and disappeared into their office, returning with a laptop. He set it on the coffee table and powered it up.

Louis turned off the television. "What's so important it couldn't wait until after New Year?"

With a few keystrokes, Pierre had an image open on the screen. "Gabriel and Annabelle haven't been able to locate Cordelia King. Maxime wants us to track her down. He said this thing with Annabelle's coven and the Faucherians was more about the Langeais wolves than we thought."

"In what way?" Louis peered at the screen. "Looks like he's sent us something out of an old manuscript."

Pierre checked his phone. "Maxime says it's from his ancestor's journal." He scrolled through the document, his eyebrows shooting up. "*Merde.*"

Louis gave a low whistle. "A time-traveling witch. And she's been targeting the Langeais wolves well before the tenth century. A worthy adversary."

Pierre grinned. "Game on." He grabbed his laptop and followed his twin to their office, cracked his knuckles and settled himself in his chair. They liked a challenge.

Louis cocked an eyebrow at him. "New Year's?"

Pierre nodded. "We'll have her before then. How hard can it be to find one little old lady?"

* * * *

Maxime swirled cognac around in his glass before draining his drink and setting the glass aside. The smooth burn of the alcohol went some way to masking his indigestion, if not the disquiet in his mind. From his desk drawer, he took out a pair of white cotton gloves and slipped them on. He opened the archival box and, with care, unwrapped the book from its protective glassine paper. His ancestor's journal, leather bound and stamped with the d'Louncrais red wax seal. Red, green and blue light bathed the journal, courtesy of Pierre's and Louis' Christmas tree. The bloody Montagne twins had insisted he get festive. Well, mostly Louis. His exuberance was more irritating than infectious.

Ignoring the tree and its bright and cheery decorations, Maxime flicked through the pages until he found the one he was looking for. At the top, the date — *the fourth day of the month of November in the year of our Lord, nine hundred and ninety-nine.* There it was, in his ancestor Gaharet d'Louncrais' bold hand. Isobella Rodriguez, belonging to the Bayside coven of San Francisco of the United States of America, daughter of Emannuel, step-daughter of Pamela Jackson and stepsister to Annabelle Jackson, mated Edmond *and* Aubert Montagne.

It was all there. How Annabelle would find the grimoire at her place of work — Rarity. That she would steal it. How she would introduce the time traveling spell to her High Priestess, Marjory Jackson, and set in action a chain of events that would lead to Isobella using the spell to go back in time to the tenth century. That Gabriel would also use the spell to save his mate, Annabelle. How, in the end, the coven would send the grimoire to the Langeais wolves. To Alain. All Maxime had needed to do was to see Rarity, and subsequently Annabelle, would get the grimoire in the first place. He'd made sure of it. He'd taken it there personally.

It would piss Gabriel off if ever he found out Maxime had known all along. At least Gabriel had his mate.

Maxime poured himself another large nip of cognac. His mate hated him. Wanted him dead. How was it possible the one woman meant for him, was one of his worst enemies?

It could be worse. He flicked a few pages ahead. Stefanie's name jumped out at him. He'd hidden this from everyone. Would have done anything for it to not be so, but if there was one thing he'd learned—fate would find a way. Gabriel and Annabelle were proof enough of that. It didn't matter if he told his sister or not. Her destiny was written right here, in his ancestor's concise hand. He needn't tell her. She would find out for herself soon enough.

* * * *

Stef dialed up her brother. She knew exactly what he'd be doing—sitting at his desk with nothing but a glass of cognac to keep him company.

"Merry Christmas, brother," she said, forcing cheer into her voice.

He grunted, and down the line came the unmistakable sound of him pouring another drink.

She sighed. "I don't know why you're wasting your time trying to get drunk, Maxime." No matter how much cognac he imbibed, his werewolf blood would always negate the effects.

"I know, but I can pretend for a little while it works."

"Why don't you go after her?" It seemed the most obvious thing to Stef. "She's your mate. Let the bond form and then...well...let nature take its course."

"Mmhm. And how would you feel if you were in her shoes? Fated to be with someone you'd been taught to despise, hmm?"

Stef bit back a retort. She knew exactly what she'd do. She'd fight it. With everything she had. And if he tried to force the issue? She'd fight harder.

"Remember this, Stef. Remember your words. There may come a time when they're more important than you can imagine."

An icy shiver rocketed up her spine. "Maxime, what are you talking about? What do you know?"

Lord knows she'd been avoiding thinking about mating anyone for quite some time now. Why on earth would she want another overbearing male in her life? She already had Maxime and Gabriel. She could barely breathe without one of them being there to witness it. And a human mate? Ugh. No thanks. But the way Maxime was talking… Like he knew who her mate was going to be, and she wouldn't like it… It was unnerving.

"I'm sorry, Stef." His weary sigh filtered down the line. "I'm feeling a little maudlin tonight. I don't mean to imply anything."

Stef couldn't sense any lie, but her brother had always been adept at concealing his emotions. "Well, don't let that go on too long. It's Christmas."

"*Oui.* I'll snap out of it. Listen, Stef. Can you do me a favor? I need you to pass on a message for me."

"Sure. Who's the message for?"

"You'll know when the time is right."

Again that sense of foreboding skittered up her spine. "Why are you being so cryptic tonight, Max? What's going on?"

Another heavy sigh. "I can't tell you, Stef. It could change things. Just memorize the message. Trust me, your brother, your alpha."

"Fine. Whatever. You and your mysterious alpha stuff." But it wasn't fine, because Stef's bullshit radar was pinging loud and insistent. "What's the message?" Maybe that would give her some clues.

"He's safe and well, and happily mated in Tasmania, Australia."

What the... "Who's safe and well?"

"I can't tell you."

Her brother's determination leaked down the phone line. She'd heard that tone many a time before. Her brother would not budge. This was all she was going to get. She tried anyway. She had a feeling it was important. Really important. "Maxime, that doesn't make any sense. How am I going to know who this message is for if I don't know who it's referring to?"

"Stefanie, know that I love you, and I've only ever wanted the best for you."

"Maxime?"

"You've been a pain in my ass, but I wouldn't change you for the world. You're a great little sister. The best. Just...don't forget everything I've taught you. Everything you've learned from Gabriel."

Stef's throat clenched. Why did this feel like a goodbye? "Don't do anything stupid, Maxime? Gabriel's staying here in San Francisco, and I'm not cut out to be alpha. Don't make me come back there and kick your ass on the training mats."

Her brother's chuckle eased some of the tightness in her chest.

"I'll take you up on that challenge, little sis. Oh, and before I forget, I've sent you a package to the hotel. It should arrive there any day now. You're going to need it. Merry Christmas, Stef."

She was going to need what, exactly? But Maxime wouldn't elaborate any further.

"Merry Christmas, Max."

Stef ended the call and stared out at the San Francisco skyline. That Maxime had had the foresight to buy this penthouse suite four years ago unnerved her. It suggested he'd known they'd be needing it. Had Alain foreseen something? Or was it about whatever was in that damn journal her brother kept locked away in his office? And now this strange message he wanted her to memorize, but he couldn't tell her why.

As soon as she returned to Saint Epain, Stef was breaking into her brother's office. She was going to read those damn journals. There was something in them about her, she was certain of it. Something she wouldn't like. Something to do with her mate.

Chapter Twenty-Five

Annabelle glanced at Gabriel's profile. Where was he taking her? They'd been driving for nearly two hours, the last half hour with their headlights cutting through the darkness. It was Christmas Eve. Gabriel had declined the invitation from her family for their traditional Christmas dinner, and they'd left Stefanie at the Ritz-Carlton.

"Almost there, *bebe*."

She peered out of the window. Nothing but forest as far as the eye could see. "Almost where?"

"*Non*. It's a surprise." The car slowed, and he flicked the indicator on. "Now, close your eyes for me."

"Really?"

He chuckled. "Come on, Annabelle. Humor me."

"All right." She grinned, then wagged her finger at him. "But this better be worth it."

She closed her eyes as they turned off the blacktop with a crunch of the tires on gravel. They were somewhere near Lake Berryessa, if her sense of direction didn't betray her.

They pulled up and he switched off the car. The icy air hit her briefly as he got out, then he was at her door helping her from the car. The engine tick ticked as it cooled, the scent of pine hung heavy in the air and branches creaked in the wintery night breeze.

He took her arm and led her from the car. "Careful now, there's three steps."

Annabelle clomped up wooden stairs, trusting Gabriel to guide her and not let her trip up. Another three steps, crossing a timber porch. A key grated in a lock, a door swung open, then she was walking into a cocoon of warmth and light. The door closed behind them with a squeak of hinges. A fire crackled, and music, Christmas carols, played softly in the background.

Gabriel stepped up behind her and wrapped his arms around her. "Remember when I said we needed time and some place private for your turning?"

Electricity zipped up Annabelle's spine, and it was all she could do not open her eyes. "Yes?"

"Well, I've cleared it with your boss. As of now, we are officially on our three-month honeymoon."

She did an excited little jig in his arms. This was happening, really happening. She'd been on edge ever since he'd stepped back into her life. Despite the last few days they'd spent together, rarely more than two feet apart from each other, and numerous declarations that he was never leaving her again, there was still a niggling doubt in the back of her mind. It'd been like this in Paris, too, and still he'd left her.

This, him staking his claim, turning her was, as far as wolf shifters went, the ultimate declaration. He'd never leave his claimed mate.

He chuckled against her ear. "I know you need this, *bebe*, but first, I owe you a Christmas, Annabelle Jackson-Rodríguez." He nuzzled her cheek. "Open your eyes, Belle."

Annabelle's eyelids fluttered open and she gasped. They were in a cozy cabin with a log fire burning in the fireplace. Tucked behind a half wall was a cute little kitchenette, a large bed with a quilted throw faced a window with a moonlit view over the lake, and in the corner, the most beautifully decorated Christmas tree she'd ever seen. She peered closer. "Are they...?"

"*Oui.*"

Dotted amongst the brightly colored baubles were the hand-carved ornaments they'd bought in Paris. Tears pricked her eyes. He'd remembered.

"I, ah, had Isobella help me with this." He cleared his throat. "Decorating Christmas trees isn't exactly the forte of the chief of security of a werewolf pack."

"It's beautiful," she whispered. She brushed at her eyes, wiping away unshed tears. "But there is one thing missing."

He looked crestfallen.

"I'll be right back."

She dashed out of the door, down the porch to the car, and grabbed her bag. Returning to the warmth of the cabin, she dug through her things and pulled out a box. Ever since Paris, it had sat in the very depths of her closet. Too precious to give away, but too heartbreaking to look at. She handed the box to him.

"What's this?" He frowned. "You bought me a present?"

She shook her head. "No. I think you may have bought me one. Back in Paris. I found it amongst all our purchases from the Christmas markets. Open it."

He opened the box and withdrew the item, peeling away the wadding to reveal a hand-blown glass star. It twinkled gold with reflected firelight.

His Adam's apple bobbed, his dark eyes full of emotion. "You kept it?"

She laid a hand on his arm. "Of course I did. You bought it for me. It was one of the few things I had left of you." Annabelle picked up her bag. "Why don't you put it on the tree, and I'll get changed into something more comfortable."

She slipped into the bathroom and stripped out of her clothes. She'd brought a few pieces of sexy lingerie, but she discarded those for something else. The gold tinsel tickled, as she threw it around her neck like a scarf, letting the end trail between her naked breasts, finishing below her belly button.

Christmas in Paris had held all the promise of their burgeoning relationship. Until he'd broken her heart by leaving her. Now here they were again on Christmas Eve, but this time Gabriel wasn't going to leave. Instead, he was handing her forever. With him. Nerves fluttered in her stomach. He was going to turn her.

He'd have to sedate her, and there were risks, but Annabelle didn't care. She wanted this. Oh, God, how she wanted it. To be claimed by him. The years ahead, with him by her side, ruling her coven. They would make up for those three years they'd lost in the years ahead. Tonight, they would have the Christmas she'd dreamed of in Paris. No longer would it be a holiday she would dread, but a reminder of her claiming.

She opened the door and leaned against the door frame. Gabriel turned, and his nostrils flared as he raked his gaze over her. A low growl rumbled in his chest.

"Merry Christmas, Gabriel."

* * * *

"Are you ready, *bebe*?"

Was she ready? On the bed, on her hands and knees, with Gabriel's big body tucked behind her and the length of tinsel long discarded, she was more than ready. Ready for his cock, and ready for his claiming. On the bedside table, there were three full syringes and a leather cuff with a silver wolf motif.

Gabriel's cock nudged her entrance. "Annabelle? Are you ready?"

"Yes." *God, yes.*

He stretched her, filling her like only Gabriel could, taking her as he knew she liked it. Hard and fast. His hands firm on her hips, he held her in place as he pounded her eager pussy.

As her orgasm rocketed through her, he flicked her hair over one shoulder and leaned his big body over her, nuzzling her neck. "Trust me, *mon amour*."

Then he bit her, large canines digging deep into her muscle. Pain and pleasure ripped through her, sending her orgasm spiraling into the stratosphere.

He released her and they collapsed onto the mattress in a sweaty, spent bundle. He pulled her close, licking the wound, sending shivers through her whole body.

"Mine. Forever," he whispered against her neck.

A deep calm settled in his chest at his words. "Yours."

It started as a tingle, radiating from his bite. Within minutes the tingle was a burn, and it was spreading, spearing deep. "Gabriel?"

Gabriel was off the bed and prepping her vein. "I've got you, *bebe*."

A sluggishness settled in her veins, and darkness tugged at the edge of her vision as Gabriel set the used syringe aside and climbed back into bed with her.

"I love you, Annabelle Jackson." He dropped a kiss on her nose. "I'll see you in three days."

Annabelle let the darkness consume her.

Epilogue

Two weeks later

"Concentrate, Annabelle."

She poked her tongue at him. "I'm trying. It's not easy, you know. It's so overwhelming. The wolf inside me is so strong. It wants to be free, to run, to chase..."

She was halfway to her feet when he moved to block her path. "*Non, non*, Annabelle. Leave the poor rabbit alone."

"But..."

There was a distinct whine in her voice, and her musky scent had deepened. Her wolf was close to the surface, pushing for a shift.

"Focus on something else."

Blue eyes, with dark indigo shadows flitting in their depths, turned to him. A growl rumbled in her chest.

He chuckled. "Not on me. You know how that ended last time."

She pouted. "I didn't hear you complaining."

His grin grew wider. "I'll never complain about having my mate in my arms, but you need to learn to control your wolf. You have a coven to run, Annabelle. And we need to prep Isobella for her journey back in time."

At the mention of Isobella, Annabelle's face clouded over. "We can't keep hiding her illness from the family, and her doctor's pushing for chemo and surgery. We have to get her to the tenth century as soon as possible. Any word from your brothers about Cordelia?"

He rubbed his hand over the stubble on his chin. "Cordelia's proving more difficult to find than we expected. She's got to have someone with some tech experience working for her. She's got identities popping up all over the world. Pierre and Louis are working day and night to crack them, but none of them are leading to anything. For all we know, she could still be here in San Francisco. Right under our noses."

"Or she's gone back to the tenth century for a stint."

He hoped not. The last thing he wanted to do was send a sick and weak Isobella back to the tenth century, only to have her encounter Cordelia.

"I was talking to Aunt Marjory yesterday about this. Every couple of years, Cordelia would vanish. She'd be gone for long stints of time. The first time it happened, she was young, in her early twenties. She disappeared again a few years later. There were suspicions she was pregnant to a warlock from a rival coven, but when she returned, she was alone.

"The same thing happened when Aunt Marjory took over the coven. She vanished again. This time for a few years. It's one of the reasons Aunt Marjory became the High Priestess. Cordelia wasn't around to challenge her. Do you think, maybe, she was going back in time?"

Gabriel considered the possibility. Annabelle's theory made a lot of sense. "If the grimoire is hers, as we suspect, it would explain why the pages are vellum and old, but the writing is in modern American English."

Worry flickered in Annabelle's eyes. "If she's back in the tenth century…"

He cupped her face. "Hey. Let's not jump to conclusions. Don't forget, Cordelia is an old lady now. That time traveling spell is brutal. As powerful a witch as she is, her body might well be too fragile to withstand it."

"I hope you're right."

"Pierre and Louis won't give up. And they're good at what they do. If she's here, in the twenty-first century, they'll find her."

"And if she's not?"

"Isobella is going to need all the training she can get before she goes. So, back to your lessons."

"Ugh." Annabelle held up her hands. "All right, all right. I know. You're talking sense." She closed her eyes, backed away from him and took in a long deep breath. "What do you want me to do?"

As tempting as it was to scoop her up in his arms and take her here on the forest floor, Gabriel called on all of his *own* training to resist the impulse. "I want you to call your wolf as close to the surface as you can. Then, holding her there, I want you to reach out with all your senses and tell me what pick you up."

"Okay." She shook herself, like an athlete preparing for the starter's gun of a race, and took a deep breath. Her body went preternaturally still, and her head tilted to the side. "The cabin. The fire's died down, but there's still smoke in the air. The lake. I can smell the lake." She gritted her teeth. "There's that rabbit again. If it knows what's good for it, it'd go away."

"Push through it, Annabelle. You can't get distracted every time some prey animal crosses your path. Turning wolf in downtown San Francisco because a pigeon flew past you, would be a real problem."

She straightened her shoulders and jutted out her chin. There was the determined Annabelle he knew.

"You can do it. Shift your focus to something else."

Her head jerked to the right. A beady-eyed raven watched them from above. Then her attention shifted, back to the rabbit, and her control slipped. Blonde hair sprouted on the backs of her hands and a large canine peeked out from beneath her top lip.

"Annabelle."

"Oh, hell."

The change roared up, and her clothes were ripping as her body shifted. Then she was off running. Gabriel shifted, heedless of another pair of torn jeans, chasing after her. Years of training, and the advantage of being a bigger wolf, had him on her heels in seconds. He launched himself at her, bringing her down in scattering of fallen pine needles. The rabbit bounded off, safe for now.

Beneath him, Annabelle's wolf retreated, leaving her bare to him with the exception of a few scraps of material. He shifted back, pinning her to the forest floor with his big body.

"I'm never going to get this," she moaned, trying to wiggle out from under him.

He nuzzled her neck. "You will, but it'll take a while, and a lot of practice."

"Something tells me you don't mind."

He grinned, nipping at the cord of her throat. "Why do you think I was looking forward to your training so much?" He trailed a fiery trail up her throat and planted a kiss on her lips.

She pushed at his chest. "You knew? That this would happen? That I'd struggle to control my form and we'd end up here? Like this? Naked? Over and over again?"

He kissed her again, briefly, but with a promise of something more to come. "Every wolf I know who's ever mated a human talks about it." He cocked an eyebrow at her. "You don't like it?" He shrugged. "We can go back to training if you like."

She wrapped her hands around his neck, holding him in place. "Hold up there, big guy. I didn't say that."

He trailed a hand up her rib cage to cup her breast. "We should get back to training.

She arched into his palm. "We should."

He rolled her nipple between his thumb and forefinger. "Isobella needs us."

Annabelle moaned. "She does, but..."

He sucked her earlobe into his mouth, then released it. "We'll be quick."

She wrapped her legs around his hips. "Yes."

He ground his hips, rubbing against her core. "Then we'll get back to training.

She gripped him tighter. "Less talking."

She captured his mouth in hers, and Gabriel lost himself to the kiss. His pack mates were right. Training was everything he'd hoped it'd be. He had an inkling things were heating up for the coven and the Langeais wolves. That Cordelia and the Faucherians wouldn't be quiet for long. Gabriel was going to revel in every last moment of this brief reprieve. After the three years they'd spent apart, he and Annabelle deserved it.

Sign up for our newsletter and find out about all our romance book releases, eBook sales and promotions, sneak peeks and FREE romance books!

Want to see more from this author?
Here's a taster for you to enjoy!

The Descendants:
The Wolves and Their Witch
K.E. Turner

Excerpt

London
April

Melinda Cheng stepped off the Tube at Baker Street station and resisted the urge to quicken her steps. With her laptop bag slung over her shoulder, she kept her pace measured and calm, the prickle on her neck not diminishing as she made her way up to the street. She was being paranoid. It was a coincidence. The events of the last three months had her on edge, seeing things that weren't there. Or maybe not. She'd learned to trust her instinct a long time ago, and it had never let her down.

The familiar façade of her building loomed, but Melinda kept walking. The last thing she wanted, if she were being followed, was to reveal where she lived. If she hadn't already.

At a boutique clothing store, with its display of the latest spring fashions, she stopped and stared at the large window. That she wouldn't be caught dead in any of this year's newest fashions was irrelevant. She ignored the clothing, focusing on the reflection of the street. Clichéd, but effective. Shoppers strolled or rushed past. An open-topped bus, half-full of tourists, momentarily blocked her view of the opposite side of the street, but he wasn't there. He hadn't followed her off the train?

She ambled past a few more shop windows and stopped again. Nope. Still couldn't see him. Maybe she *had* been imagining things. But… London was home to millions of people. What were the chances of running into the same man three times in one day?

She casually spun around, as though trying to decide which shop might interest her. Still no sign of him. If he hadn't looked like he'd stepped off the pages of some magazine, or a billboard advertisement for Calvin Klein, she might not have noticed him. No. She would've noticed him. There was a sense of danger about him that couldn't be ignored, no matter how handsome he was. She would've picked him out of a crowd of one hundred thousand or more. Her radar to dangerous men had been tuned since childhood.

As though on impulse, Melinda stepped into a bakery. With a quick glance at the patrons to make sure *he* wasn't one, she placed an order to go and waited by the counter, keeping a close eye on the people walking past. With how she earned her money, there was always a risk. Some of her clients weren't the altruistic kind.

But she was certain this was about one in particular. One who had more in common with the women she helped than those she used for income. Username — MysticMage. Based on the photo sent to Melinda, she was an octogenarian. On the dark web. That was a first. For her, at least. Most of the clients she helped were much younger.

MysticMage hadn't *said* it was a husband she was running from, but Melinda had recognized the signs.

She'd read between the lines. Four times she'd created a new identity for her, only to have someone crack it wide open. For goodness' sake, the woman was in her eighties. Couldn't her husband let her live out the last few years of her life in peace? Obviously not, because when they'd hacked Melinda's fifth attempt at creating her a new identity, the hacker had done something else. He'd sent malware through her triggers.

She'd been out of her chair, ripping out the router cable and shutting the computer down within seconds. Had she been fast enough? Had he got enough information to track her location? For there could be no other reason for the malware. She'd been jittery ever since.

Maybe she needed to take a holiday. Tell MysticMage she'd need to find another hacker and go somewhere warm and sunny, with white beaches and blue water. Where no one would think to look for her. Somewhere like the Greek Islands. She'd always wanted to go.

No. She'd promised she'd keep her client safe, and she was going to damn well do her job. She'd need to take extra precautions, that's all. And back trace that malware without giving up more than she already had. Then she'd send him a nasty little virus of her own for his trouble.

She accepted her tea, turned to leave, and froze. At the counter was *the* guy. There was no mistaking him. Black Henley stretched across a broad chest, snug jeans hugging muscular thighs, the bronzed skin, the dark hair curling at his nape. Like a Spanish sex God. Or a celebrity. As he perused the cake display, the young female server grinned at Melinda and winked, mistaking her open-mouthed stare for interest.

She snapped out of her trance and waggled her eyebrows at the server, giving the Spanish sex god the once over. Not because she was admiring the taut, rounded globes of his ass, but because she was looking for something that might give her a hint to his identity. A gang tattoo, or…or a leather cuff about his wrist with the silver motif of a… Was that a wolf or a dog?

Okay, maybe she lingered a little on his ass. Before he noticed her staring, she smiled again at the server and walked past the Spanish hottie as though he were nothing more than a momentary distraction.

She dumped her tea in the trash and hurried across the street to a bookstore, browsing the recent releases, her attention fixed not on any book, but on the bakery entrance. The guy with the perfect ass exited, coffee and a paper bag in hand, and turned down the street away from her building. *Huh.* Maybe she was being overly suspicious of him. Seeing him four times in one day *could* be a coincidence. If he lived in the neighborhood. She'd never seen him before, though. She shook her head. This business with the malware had her spooked.

After a few more turns down the street and no further sighting of the hottie, Melinda entered her building. In the empty lift, she leaned against the back wall, letting the tension ease from her shoulders. A nice cup of jasmine tea would go down well. She had a mind to whip up a quick stir-fried egg with tomato. *Mm, yeah.* Her stomach rumbled.

The door was almost closed when a hand and wrist, with a leather cuff and silver motif, shoved between them and the door bounced back open. Melinda stiffened.

Get the hell outta here.

Six-foot something of black Henley and snug jeans smiled perfect white teeth at her. "Thought I was going to miss it."

A thick accent... Not Spanish, though she could have sworn he had at least some Spanish or Latino heritage. French, maybe? He glanced at his watch as he and a waft of spicy aftershave joined her in the lift. She resisted the temptation to breathe him in. A man who was potentially stalking her shouldn't smell that good.

Melinda smiled back, her hand tightening around the strap of her bag. She adjusted her glasses, partially hiding her face as her gaze skimmed over him. Had his hair been a smidge longer? The shadow of a stubble on his chin darker? Numbers glowed from the control panel, but it was the watch on his wrist when he leaned over to punch the button to close the doors that held her attention. A platinum Roger Dubuis Excalibur. She hadn't noticed *that* in the bakery. Strange.

The doors slid shut before she could will her feet to move.

"What floor?" he asked.

He raked a hand through his hair. The action, the stretching of his shirt, the tautening of a bicep... *Is it hot in here?* She wanted to fan her super-heated face. Her attention snagged again on that watch.

She cleared her throat. "Um, eight," she lied. "Thank you."

His eyebrows pinched together. "Are you sure?" His hand hovered over the control panel.

She lifted her chin. "Yes. Sorry, long day."

With a shrug, he punched floor eight and floor nine. *Nine.* Her real floor.

He leaned against the elevator wall, hazel eyes framed by long lashes no man deserved to be born with, giving her the once over. Bedroom eyes. Cute.

Smoldering. An image of him, naked, tangled in her sheets, rose unbidden.

What the hell, Melinda?

They stood in silence, Melinda staring at the numbers lighting up as the lift rose, the weight of his stare burning holes in the side of her face.

Why is the lift so damn slow today?

She risked another peek. The man could be a bodyguard, with all that muscle. Or a bouncer. Or an underwear model. He'd look good in nothing but a pair of boxer briefs. That bronze skin, the dark shadow on his jaw. Would he have a happy trail?

Or... He could be a private investigator, or a thug sent to intimidate the location of her client out of her.

Or not. Those jeans were snug, and there was no evidence he was concealing a weapon. Her gaze dipped to his crotch. She doubted he'd be hiding a gun there. At least, not the type of gun she was imagin— She cut the thought off, sucking in a deep breath of aftershave.

He pushed himself off the wall, and her gaze followed the flex of muscles across his abdomen up his chest and... *Oops. Busted.* Heat crept up her neck, and she turned away, but not before she caught the flare of his nostrils, and... Was that a...*growl*?

The lift dinged, lurched to a halt, and the door slid open. Melinda dipped her head at him, escaped the confined space and strode down the corridor as if she did, truly, live on this floor. As soon as the lift doors slid shut, she raced for the stairs. Above her, a door closed, then she was alone in the cool stairwell.

With her laptop on the top step and the click of a few commands, Melinda logged into her secure wireless router and pulled up the security feed from the ninth floor.

There he is.

Without a glance at her door, he continued down the corridor to one at the end. *Huh.* Old Mrs. Bellamy had moved out last week. Her kids must have finally put her into that care home they'd been pushing for. He *wasn't* following her? He was her new *neighbor?*

On the grainy security feed, he shifted his coffee and his pastry bag to one hand and retrieved his key.

Wait. What?

Melinda froze the image. He held a takeaway coffee cup and a pastry bag. And there, as obvious as the bulge in his pants had been, was a naked wrist. This *wasn't* the guy in the lift. He wasn't wearing an Excalibur watch.

What the hell?

She tapped a few keys and unfroze the image. Mr. No-Watch was gone—the door to Mrs. Bellamy's flat closed—but striding down the hall *was* the guy from the lift. Mr. Excalibur. She heaved out a sigh. Twins. Her new neighbors, they were twins. But the question remained—what was a man doing living in this building when he could afford to spend two hundred and fifty thousand pounds on a *watch*?

About the Author

K.E. Turner can't remember a time when she wasn't writing stories or reading books — as a teenager in class instead of doing math, in her lunch break at work, or at home when there's housework to be done. With a love of history, mystery, suspense, paranormal, and romance, she likes combining more than one element in her stories.

An award winning author, she writes spicy paranormal romances and romantic suspense, with strong but good hearted heroes, smart, sassy heroines and an often unexpected villain or two, to shake things up.

A Western Australian based author, she lives with her husband, two dogs, two cats and a menagerie of farm animals on their property in the southern region of the state. A hopeless romantic, she enjoys beach sunsets, sitting by the wood fire with a good book, a nice shiraz and good food.

K.E. Turner loves to hear from readers. You can find her contact information, website details and author profile page at https://www.firstforromance.com

ENTWINED PUBLISHING